George William Bagby

**Original letters of Mozis Addums to Billy Ivvins**

George William Bagby

**Original letters of Mozis Addums to Billy Ivvins**

ISBN/EAN: 9783337135737

Printed in Europe, USA, Canada, Australia, Japan

Cover: Foto ©Andreas Hilbeck / pixelio.de

More available books at **www.hansebooks.com**

# Mozis Addums to Billy Ivvins,

—BY—

## DR. GEO. W. BAGBY,

AUTHOR OF

"What I Did with My Fifty Millions," "Meekins's
Twinses," &c., &c.

New and Revised Edition, with an Introduction and Notes.

Richmond:
*Printed for the Author by Clemmitt & Jones.*
1878.

# INTRODUCTION.

In 1857, I went to Washington to take the place of my friend Wm. M. Semple, as correspondent of the *New Orleans Crescent*. Two letters a week to the *Crescent*, and three to the *Eagle and Enquirer*, a Memphis paper, left me plenty of leisure for other writing. I had never attempted anything in what is called "Dialect," but, having a natural turn for bad spelling, thought I would try my hand. Accordingly, I sent the first letter of Mozis Addums to Billy Ivvins to John R. Thompson, who was then editing the *Southern Literary Messenger*. He printed it, not without misgivings, and its success amazed both of us, for it was copied all over Virginia, and in many papers outside the State. I literally "woke up and found myself famous," much to my annoyance, for I was then ambitious to succeed in quite other and more elevated fields of literature. But the public would have its way. From that day to this I have gone by the name of "Mozis," and I am sure that, directly and indirectly, these letters have paid me better than all my other writings put together.

Wm. Cullen Bryant complained in his later years that "Thanatopsis," a production of his youth, overshadowed all his subsequent efforts, however labored and meritorious. With much better reason, if I may be permitted to name myself in such company, may I complain that my best exertions have still left me plain "Mozis Addums," a name that for many years made me a little sick whenever I heard it. But at length I got used to it, and now that age and thwarted ambition have brought me humility, I say to myself, "Well, it is something to have a name at all, provided it is not a bad one."

The reader must judge for himself, whether the fact be or be not creditable to the popular taste, but it is a fact that the letters of Mozis Addums added several hundred names to the subscription list of the *Messenger*, while the "Reveries of a Bachelor," by Ik Marvel, which appeared originally in the same magazine, made no impression whatever until they were printed in book form, when they at once established the author's reputation as a man of letters, and paved the way to fortune.

Messrs. West & Johnston published a small edition of the Letters in 1862, but they were sold mostly to soldiers in the field, and were soon lost or destroyed.

Washington, when Mozis first saw and described it in 1857, presented a very different aspect from what it does now. Its population was not half so large; the immense improvements in the grading, &c., of the streets had not been even imagined; Boss

Shepherd was a little boy; the great sectional war was indeed contemplated, but as a thing of the remote future ; and the consolidation of the Republic into a Nation, with a permanent capital, destined to become an imperial city, was, to say the least, problematical.  While the streets were undisturbed, the public buildings, including the capitol, were being enlarged, and upon their summits were to be seen the derricks and cranes which Mozis likened to the triggers of immense partridge traps.  The House was in the new hall, but the Senate sat in its old chamber, and the Supreme Court occupied an ill-lighted room in the basement just below.  Congress was in the throes of the Kansas-Nebraska excitement, the Democratic party was insisting upon the right of slaveholders to carry their slaves into the territories, the Republicans were resisting this right, and the struggle between the sections was rapidly approaching its final issue.— Strange! it now seems, that men did not see and prepare for it.

Most of the characters who figure in these letters are real. Some of them have passed away, but, considering the length of time that has elapsed since the letters were written, a surprising number remain.  The "beautiful little girl from Indiana" has left two charming daughters who are nearly grown.  "Oans," the dearest friend that Mozis had, in spite of the jokes that he practised on him, has his place in life filled by two manly boys and a lovely girl; but the "Trungils," including their father, who is distinguished for his political writings, are all living; so are the "two pretty married ladies," and so is the "bald-headed gentleman," who is now the president of a large and flourishing college. The "Mince-Pie" or Avenue House, long ago ceased to be a hotel; the rooms that "Mozis" and "Melloo" occupied on Seventh street are used for purposes of trade, their landlady has retired on a competency, I believe; the Congressmen who entertained Mozis with their dreams of power and purposed dispensing of offices when they should become President, are no longer known in political life; and, in a word, the flight of time has brought upon Washington and its inhabitants the usual changes. I wonder if to those who have survived these changes, there is, as to the writer, the usual disappointment in life, the shortcoming in aspirations. So far as fortune and reputation in certain pursuits are concerned, many of them, I am glad to say, have succeeded; but I doubt if any one of them has achieved just the success which he then anticipated and desired. One of the Congressmen, I know, had every right to expect a political career of the greatest brilliancy, but has become a railroad president, rich, politically unknown, and perhaps all the happier for being unknown.

See Notes at end of volume.

G. W. B.

*Richmond, Dec'r, 1878.*

# LETTERS

OF

# MOZIS ADDUMS TO BILLY IVVINS.

## FIRST LETTER.

FROM FOMVIL TO WASHINTUN, BY WAY OF RICHMUN.

WASHINTUN CITY, Dec. the 14, 1857.

*To* MISTER BILLY IVVINS,
*Kerdsvil, Buckingame Cty, Ferginny.*

DEAR BILLY:
You reclect lass summer arfter I had puffectid my skeam and had detummined to go to Washintun city, I promist you to rite freekwently if not oftner, and to giv you a acount uv all I seen and dun. Well, I've bin hear more'n a weak, and has writ nar time yit, for the resin that I has seen so much, aud bin so busy I kudint think, much mo rite. Billy, this ar the dirndest place on the fase uv the erth. But I'm a goin to begin at the beginin.

I took the car at Fomvil on Fridy, a onlucky day. It were the fust time uvver I took the car, but I warnt skeered, becos I had seen the car a menyer time befo. The sensashun preduced upon the mine ar that uv rapid travlin, but no man, I doant keer how good a rethmetishun he is, kin count the pannils uv the fense a goin along.   But the mile stones aint like it was in a grave-yard; that's a lie, and aludes to the telegraf posses.   The High Bridge did'nt skeer me nuther, and I wunder it skeer ennybody, fur the injine goes over it so slow that ef the blame thing was to bust thoo, we'd all be ded befo we could pos'bly git akrost.   Bimeby we reecht the Junkshin, whar I techt about three fingers uv ball-fase whisky which I kinnot admier it.   Nuvver do you mend yo drink at the Junkshin.

Leevin uv the Junkshin, my hed a buzzin with the striknine whisky, we got upun the Damvil rode, and thar the car farly ript it along, going a bumblin like litenin upon what they call the strop rail, which ar not a sollid rail, sich as they have on the Sowthside rode, but nuthin mo nor less than a waggun tire nailed doun to a rarfter.

I notist that the peepel in the car sot their eyes on me mighty keen, and fur a time I was alarmd, feerin I had let loose my skeam which corntinually orkupide my mine.   But it was nuthin but the atentshun which a stranjer naterally adtracks.   I shill not dwell upon the minushee uv the jerney: sufice it to say, that, twards dark, we bulged down frum the piney ole feelds and the cole pitts to the ruvver, which we skeerted with rapidity, the injine settin up a loud shout as we went howlin into the toun uv Richmun. Plegg take them bridgis! it takes no less than fo bridgis to cross the ruvvur at this pint, and you ketch a site uv toun jest in time to git intoo a nuther bridge and see nuthin.

Billy, I kin not furgit the howr I enterd Richmun.   Ef the fac uv it bein the fust time I had paid my visit to a toun of great dimenshuns hadint bin the fac, the okashun wood still have bin momentious and foevver imprest itself upon my memry, from this suckumstunce. I wus skeered too deth—litrilly, and no jokin, skeerd too deth !

Skeerd? Mozis Addums don't git skeerd about nuthin. But I wuz tho'. I sot thar trimblin and sweatin, not knowin whether to move han nor fut, wharas the rest snatched up thar little um-brellers and things and put out like a gang uv wile turkies. I didn't budge. Sertny, I felt my insignifgunce in the midst uv them thousings uv rich merchonts and educated peepul, not knowin nar, single, livin ι uv 'em. But twarnt that that skeerd me, Billy, and I warnt afeard that somebody was goin to hert me, for I has bonier nuckles than most men, and you no the size uv the frog in my arm. It were the all-fired, the owdashus, and tre-menjus noise that skeer'd me. It wus enuf to uv skeered me. May be you've heerd two injines hollerin at wunst. You've heerd the wind bellorin in the woods like a bull travlin to a cuppen thoo a bresh pile, and peepul shoutin at camp meetin and 'lectshuns, and crows holdin uv a debatin sciety in the evenin. You've hearn them things. Also you've knode the devil to git into the fowils. and the turkees git to gobblin, and the geese to cacklin, and the Ginny chickins to havin uv the hiccups all at the same time, hard as they kin stave. Well, jest imagin all them noises tangled up like a fishin line and comin right slap into yo' nakid ear when you did'nt pretend to ixpec it. Taint nuthin, taint beginnin to be nuthin cumpard with what I heerd when the car stopt in Rich-mun. And what you reckin this horrid rackit wuz when I come to find it out? Why, it precedid frum a passel—I don't think thar wus mo'n two duzen uv 'em, but I kudent see strait at the time—a bout two duzen uv the wust, the durndest, sassiest, big-mouthdist carridge drivers hollerin at the peepel to git to carry thar things, trunks and so foth, to the tavuns. Nuver, nuver, did I heer the beet uv it. It mighty nigh distractid me—and I has sense bin told that thar is forty odd deef peepul in Richmun and 9 in the loomatick from them very carridge drivers—but, for some reesin or ruther, I spose thar is a reesin, they calls a car-ridge in toun a hac. May be the carridges thar is made uv hac-berry. I don't no. But them plegg-goned drivers ought to be whipt day and nite, pennytenchrid in fac.

Kunsultin the importunce uv my skeam, and havin heerd uv the place befo, I went into the crowd uv them drivers all hollerin "take yo' baggige, sir;" "carridge, sir: "hac, sir;· "Poter fur the Sin Charles;" "Poter fur the Merrykin;" "Poter fur the Ix-chain;" went right into 'em; and havin getherd my sensis, grad-yully discuvered the nigger uv the Ixchain and kollerd him.

Sais I, "I want to go right home with you."

Sais he, very plitely, "gimme yo' chex, yung marster," and I not knowin the meenin uv chex, follud whar he pintid, untwel I cum to a splendid, paintid kind uv a sirkus waggin with a heep uv winders and reel velvit seets on the sides, and steps to git up at the hind part uv it. But the Ixchain nigger he cum right behine me, and got arfter me agin 'bout my chex. Billy, the very devil wuz to play, and I mighter knowd it fur startin on Fridy. I can't take no time to tell you what chex is. Think I hadn't lef my confoundid ole trunk, mar's best har trunk, at the Junkshin? Fust I wuz distrest, becos I thought I were lost, fur you know what wuz in that trunk wuth munny; then I snortid and kavortid and cussd mysef into vulger frackshins. In the eend I paid a

telegraf to the Junkshin, and the cussid trunk come down the
rode the nex morning befo day.

The Ixchain ar a magnifeeshint bildin. Thar is two uv 'em,
knectid by a bridge, which spangs the street, and which is better'n a' house in Buckingame county. One side the street is filled
with 1 hous, and the other side is filled with the other hous: the
bridge jines 'em, is I sed. The hous on this side has pillers
higher'n a tree, and the hous on that side has, I recken, more'n a
thousun winders. All Fomvil could git in that tavun, and it not
feel it. Inside the hous, Billy, it jest dazzles you right up. Marbul floes, laid in dimunds; lamps uv solid gold, hangin doun like
the branchis uv a white oke, and lightid with what they call gas,
a kind uv nuthin, like the ar, that smells very loud when it aint
lightid, but when it is burnin makes every thing like broad day.
Then thar is lookinglassis, framed in gold, big is the side uv a
con-hous, and picktchers and paintins, and a splendid bar-room
and a dinin room filled with tables, and mo niggers and people
and trunks and hacs and sirkus waggins, (which is called hominy
busses,) comin and goin and talkin and smokin and drinkin and
eatin and chawin tobacker and goin up stars and a comin doun
and ringin uv bells, than you uver heerd uv. I koodent eat
nothin the night I got thar, for lookin. They've got a thing thar
to tell when supper is reddy which it is called a gon, a round
peece of sheet-iun, a little bigger'n the hed uv a flowr barril. A
nigger comes along holdin uv the thing in one han' by a string
uv twine, and in the other han' he's got a kunsern with a handil
sumthin like the handil uv a skroo driver with the little eend uv
it stuck into a trabball. He knox the gon with the trabball, and I
jes' tell you it soun's mo' like the day uv jedgment wuz comin

than ennything I uver heerd. When I fust heerd it, my har riz up like the teeth uv a wool card, and I was a heep mo' skeered than when the carridge drivers was a hollerin so at the deep O. But seein no body didn't mine it, I nuvver let on, and you is the fust i I has sed a werd too about it. Don't tell enny of them boys at Kurdsvil 'bout it. I koodent help thinkin' what a fine thing that ar gon would be to skeer crows out uv a confeel with.

I went to bed rite erly, for my eyes wus a akin and my hed a sizzin. Mr. Ballud, the tavun-keeper, was mighty kine and per-lite. Says he, "Mr. Addums, I am a goin to put you in a high posishun, whar you kin see everything." Says I, "I'm obleeged to you," and I follered a nigger up stars untwel we went cleen out ov site, and he put me in a long, narrer room, with a roun win-der whar I could see, when day come, the tops ov a millyun uv houses with the smoke risin out uv the chimbleys and a peese uv the ruver which rose* in the nite like a liun. The washstan uv the room was reeal mogny, but it didn't have no marbul top sich as I has sense seen, the cheers wus good cheers, nuthin extry, thar wuz a carpit on the flo, no fire plais (but it warnt cole) and the bed mighty low doun to the groun, like a trundil bed. I likes a bed that stan's up like a man: sqotty beds soots wimmen and fellers that's drunk and draps whar they falls, 'thout ondressin. But the sheets was linnin and dlishus. The pillars is too big— give me a little, easy, sortor mushy pillar all the time.

It took me nigh onto a our to git to sleep, and then I didn't sleep, but kep a wakin and a jumpin, my hart beetin, and I a thinkin about my trunk and what wuz in it. You kno. It come

* Mr. Addums means roars.

in the mornin', is I told you befo, and it wuz thar, safe and soun inside the trunk. Nobody had'nt tetched it.

Billy, the peepul in Richmun nuvver sleep. Oftin as I jumpt up in bed in the nite, they wuz comin' and goin, travlin up and doun the passagis, treddin on the heals uv thar bootes and makin uv too much noise. The Lord only nose what they wuz a doin, and how they does to do without sleep beets my time. Kuntry peepul is bleest to sleep some, and me ptickly. I don't see no use uv havin up beds ef peepul don't sleep.

'Bout lite, or a little arfter, I got up, washt my fase, and eet brekfus with the passinjus goin on the car. Tried to git a tansy dram befo I eet, but they did'nt have none at the bar, fine as it wuz. Enyhow, I had a appytight, and laid in some 9 spar rib with aags to match,—etcetry. Smokt a fine seegar at 4punce to keep up my ca'ickter, but had ruther uv had a pipe with some plane trash* at nuthing atall.

Holdin up my puppus in vue, I throde away about a inch and a half uv my seegar and set to biznis. Fust I inquide fur the Guvner. They tole me, but tole me not to go thar untwel 10 o'clock, and plegg take it all, I had to wait. Well, the Guvner lives in a right deasant sort uv a squar hous in one cornder uv the Captul Yard, and when I got thar at 10 o'clock he warnt thar. So I asked for ole Mr. Richy, whar he lived, and they tellin me, and I folrin uv thar dreckshins got into Main street, whar thar was so menny sines and things that I got lost. Then I sees a young man, a dark complected feller he were, and had 1 uv them

* Crumbled tobacco.

swelled faces that comes uv drinkin uv whisky or havin uv the
tooth-ake.  I sais to him, I sais:

"Kin you tell me whar the Inquirer Offis is, whar Mr. Richy
lives?"

And he lookin uv me plum in the eye, sais nuthin.  Pres'ntly
he remarkt, he sais, very perlite, sais he:

"You see that ar tall hous over thar with the flag a flyin from
the pole?"  I sais, "yes."   "Well," he sais, "that's the Merrikin
hotel, and you jes go down the side uv it till you cum to anuther
pole, something like that on top the hotel, only the flag aint thar,
but the streaks uv the flag is ropt round the pole, painted like.
That's the Inquirur Offis, certin.

I goes down, and when I gits to the pole, I knox.  They sais
"cum in," and openin uv the winder I sees a heap uv lookin
glasses, two or three likely m'latter boys, with kombs in thar har
and apurns on, and a fellow standin befo a glass tying uv sumthin
round his neck.

"Ar this the Inquirur Offis?" I sais.

The m'latter boys they lafft, but the fellow at the glass sais,

"Yes, this is the Inquirur offis.   What kin we do for you?" he
sais.

"I want to see the editer."

"Well, he aint here."

"Whar is he?"

"He's ded and berrid—berrid bout a fortnit ago."

That flustrated me a good eel, and I didn't know what to do,
but jest to be sayin sumthin, I sais:

"What did he die uv?"

"Well," he sais. "I can't say that I igzackly know, but ef you want to subscribe, I'll take yo munny jest as ef he wus livin."

I tole him, "No, I dinn't rede mighty well, and hadn't no munny to spar."

With that follerd a considerbul uv talk betwixt us; he apeerin very ankshus to fine out my biznis, and I not lettin on. I has sense learnt that that warnt no Inquirur Offis atall, but a barber's shop. So I didn't see the Guvner, nor Mr. Richy nuther.

Arfter I left the barber's shop, I reckin I went into 20 bar rooms looking fur editers, and bein constuntly fooled; fur the peepul uv Richmun has no better sense than to think it mighty funny to fool foax from the kuntry. But I did git to see sum editers, and had some chat with um, but as I wus afraid to let out about my skeam, I didn't learn nuthin what I wantid.

Bein satisfide I couldn't do no biznis, I startid roun to see the curostis. They told me Rockits were a pritty plais, and I went thar, and seen a number uv sale vessils, which is amuzin to a man that nuver seen nun befo, but aint so mighty pritty nether. The merchunt's mills, in my opinyun, is the best lookin things in Richmun. By George! they is busters. Billy, thar is mo brik in one uv them mills than in Fomvil and Ciry put together.

I heerd thar was some fine grave yards in the sububs uv the sitty, but I didn't go to nun uv um, prefearing a sirkus, which thar want enny in town.

The Captul bildin, whar they make the lors, aint is hansum is the Ixchain. Inside uv it thar is a likeniss in white rock uv Ginrul Washintun, with a kane in his han and a plow pint, and sum mo things at his feet. I seen no ubjeckshun to this likeniss, exceptin they have drawd his stock ruther tite, givin uv a choked

look to him. On the fur side uv the Captul I found two tremendus brass men, histed on the bottom part uv the banisters uv the
steps. One was Potric Henry, and the uther wus Tom Jeffsun.
Potric Henry wus a orrytur, and Tom Jeffsun he was the fust
dimmycrat, 'cept one, which is Abyham, which didn't beeleve in
no guvermint atall, but went wharuver he durn pleased and didn't
pay no taxis.

In lookin at these gentilmen, I wuz struck by the fac how much
bigger peepul used to be than they is now. And I atributed the
fallin off on our part to the use of bad sperits.                    ,,

Goin on a leetil further from the brass men, is what they calls
the Washintun monumint, and on the rite side uv it the biggest
box I uver heerd uv, tilted up agin the monumint. Inside uv this
box they tole me wus anuther likeniss uv Ginrul Washintun,
straddlin uv a rarrin hoss. I reflectid apun the suckumstunce a
good eel, and cum to the detuminéation that ef the ole Ginrul wus
alive to see the wickidniss uv these times, he'd be rarrin instid uv
his hoss. But I dunno,—peepul always thinks these times is
wuss'n them times.

Thar is a crowd mo uv things, Billy, to tell you uv in Richmun, but I shill not till you uv um now. When we all gits together agin, I shill tell you. But the wust uv it all cum about by my
runnin aroun to see the things, and the fust thing I node it wer
nite. I had dun miss my dinnir, which they made me pay fur it
all the same like I had eet it. This is cheeting uv the wust kine.
But Mr. Ballud he didn't seem to agree with me on this pint.
But he didn't make nuthin out'n me at supper. I jest tell you I
laid in a kord.

That big red-face feller which invegild me into the barbershop in the mornin, he was thar, and sot right acrost the tabil frum me. Seein uv me how I eet, he spoke up mighty peart, he sais:

"You don't seem to have no appytight."

I sais to him, "No, and ef I didn't have no mo appytight than you've got mannus, livin would be cheap whar I wus."

I sed this mighty perlite and meely-moutht, but he seein uv a kind uv a growl in my eye, shet up.

Arfter awhile I wus out on the steps smokin uv a seegar, he cum at me agin. I wus lonesum, and warnt sorry he cum.

ᴵᴵ"Stranjer in the city, I pesume," he sais.

I sais, "Yes."

S'e, "Buying uv goods?"

S'I, "No."

S'e, "Leave yo fam'ly well?"

S'I, "Tollibul, I thank you."

S'e, "I woodent take you to be a marrid man, ser, you look mighty young."

S'I, "You rite. I aint marrid yit."

Arfter that he did'nt say no mo for sum time. Peard like he wus studyin about sumthin. Presn'ly he commenst agin, he sais:

S'e, "Goin back to Fluvaner in the mornin?"

S'I, "I thank you, ser, I don't live in no sich place as Fluvaner, and I aint a going back in the mornin. I'm a travlin."

S'e, "Fur yo helth?"

S'I, "Skeersly"

He shet up agin. Pritty soon—

S'e, "Sold yo mules?"

S'I, " How in the name o' sense did you kno I had eny mules?"

S'e, "Oh, we foax in town nose everything.  Did you git a good prise?"

S'I, "Only far—well, frum far to middlin'?"  But how he uver come to kno about them mules I sold your par is a mistry to me. He walkt off like he was goin away, but all of a suddin he turned roun and sais:

S'e, "How'd you like to take a little turn this ev'nin?"

S'I, "Turn at what?"

S'e, "Tapistry, velvit."

S'I, "I don't ketch yo meenin."

S'e, "Gran plazzer, copper in the vessil, f'roshus animil in the jungil.  You kno."

S'I, "Mistur, I don't understan French, and you kno it, and ef you think you're goin to redikewl me, you'll find you've got the rong sow by the year.  I'm a mighty chicken-harted man, but thar is some things I won't put up with, as you'll find out pritty durn quick ef you keep a foolin arfter me " ½

Then he beg'd my pardin—sed he didn't meen to hurt my feelins, and all that.  But I told him to clear out, I did'nt want no more to do with him.  And I did'nt, for you kno, Billy, that when I'm mad I'm mad.

That was the last I seen uv him, and the last advencher I had in Richmun, from which I shuck off the dust uv my feat the follorin mornin, taking the North car a leetil arfter sun up.

But what do you expect "f'roshus animil in the jungle" is?

Why, it stan's for "tiger," which is the name of a cheetin' gaim uv keerds, which you gits chawed up by it, like a tiger had holt of you.  And that feller that got after me wuz what they calls a "stewed pidgin'," or sumethin' like that, which I never knowed befo' that cooked vittles agreed with tigers. But even squobs is onhelthy to most peepul, much mo' tigers. I know'd a 'oman that mighty nigh died uv squob, and didn' eet but bar'ly ·seven at a time neither.

Yo afecks'nit fren, trooly,

MOZIS ADDUMS.

·

## SECOND LETTER.

WASHINTUN.  MR. ADDUMS FINDS IT DIFFICULT TO OBTAIN BODE.

DEAR BILLY:

Thar is two ways uv goin' frum Richmun to Washintun; uv coas I took the rong way. Ef you go by one way, you kin see Mount Vurnun in a steembote whar Ginrul Washintun were born; on the other rode, its all rode and no water. It follers that I didn't lay ize on the berth plais uv the farther uv his country, but went along all day untwell we cum to Ellicksandry, a toun that ridin a hominbus thru doant apeer to be much. Ruther dry, ruther dry, and fitteegin to live in fer enny length uv tiem I should say. As fer bizness, I rekin its a right peert place, jedgin from the sale vessils in the ruver, and the best uv peepul live thar on nothin' a year.

To git to Ellicksandry, you got fust to git on the Centrul rode and then on the Orringe rode, which it brings yew finally to the pint; passin sum po, flat lan, and agin a trac uv tip-top rollin country, with mountings in the distans. Besides the lan and the rode running strait is a arrer, thar aint so mighty much to reckmend this rowt, ixceptin it ar wun thing: Billy, konshentshusly, thar kin mo pritty gearls be seen on this rode then I reckin in the hole wirld, and it bein uv a good thing to see um enny tiem, it ar p'tickly so in cummin to Washintun, which it is the po'ist plais for pritty gearls I uver seen, and that's sayin uv a heap for a man born and raist on Willis's. Thar is a appinted time evry day for the cars to past the deepos, and knowin uv this the gearls asembils thar in sich numbus and vriety that it acurd to me that thar must be a bodin school evry ten miles along the rode. Certny, from sum caws, thar is a cuyus klectshin uv luvli yung wimmin at these pints.

Leevin Ellicksandry, you takes a steembote, the fust I were uver on, havin seen wun at Rockitts a good eel biggern this wun. Oneesy way uv traveling are a steembote, which it shakes with venjints in its innards all the tiem, like it had a agur; and the water below weighs you down in yo' mind, becaws ef the consern gits blode up, it is boun to droun you certin, ixceptin you wuz a mity good swimmer, which I ain't being subjic to the cramps uv the legs in a ordnerry milpon. It's 7 miel to Washintun on the kontinyully tremblin steembote, but it dont look nigh so fur up the river, which it is broad here is* a hundud Appymattuxes at Fomvil, and nuthin to intrupt the view but a few passin sale vessils.

The steembote skufflin along the buzzum uv the P'tomuck like a snaik dockter, I stud and lookt at Washintun, and lookt at it, and lookt at it. Billy, it shines in the distans uv a wintry evenin with a strange sort uv look. Thar it is, the grate big sitty stretcht out upon the ground, with splended bildins and steeples and monyumints, lookin like a picktcher, which you know is reel; and how all uv it got thar, you don't know; and who's thar, and what's goin to bekum uv you thar, you don't know; and you

---

* Mister Addums frequently uses " is " in place of " as,"

feel sorry for yourself, home is so fur away, tho you left it like yistiddy.   How it is with uther peepul, I can't say, but with me goin
into a big sitty is atendid with a sense uv fear and danger, which
is vague, and all the worse for bein so.   The housis look mitey
fine, but the sky over the sity and back uv it is dark and distrest.
But the bottim part of the sky evrywhar is sad, evin in the mornin
at sun up, ef you look at it good.    I don't understand it. Iᐟ

Seein Washintun in the ginrul, you don't know what you see,
unless thar is sumbody thar to tell yew.   I were too much ockyu-
pied lookin, I didn't ass no questuns.   What most ingaged my
atenshun was the marvel bildins, and a thing that when I cum
to find it out were anuther Washintun monyumint, the same
as that in Richmun, bilt in memory uv Ginrul Washintun, only
this wun is a heep higher and diffrintly shapt.   A tremenjus tall,
squar post of white rock, this wun is ; with the frame uv a meat
hous on top uv it.   It sets on the ruver bank, and a lonesomer,
outlandisher thing you can't imagine.   It taint finisht yit by a
long shot.   They tell me its to be 600 feet high, and were risin
rapidly untwell the No-Nuthins got hold uv it and stopt it, sense
which nobody goes anear it, and it stans thar like the pizen tree
we read uv in jografy which peepul are afeard to breethe the ar
in the naborhood uv it.   I declar pintedly, it ar a shame for the
Amerrykin peepul to do in this way.                    •

Next to the desertid monyumint, my mine was drawd to the
Capitul—Capitul uv the hole United States; a supub eddyfiss
which I wont discribe at this tiem.   The reesin why I dont it aint
finisht.   In fac, Billy, nuthin aint finisht in this toun, ixcept it is
roskallity, which it is the only thing thar is no need uv eny futher
apropriashuns for the ixtenshin uv.

When the bote recht the warf, (warf is sum bodes nailed down on sum stobs stuck in the bottum uv the ruver, runnin out from the bank, whar you stop and hitch the bote and git off at,) thar insude another seen, as the Him Book says, uv kunfewshun and creecher cumplaint, with hax, and hac-drivers holrin, and homny-busses and peepul gittin off, sumthin like at the deep O in Richmun, but not so bad and terryfine to a body. Now I didnt kno nuthin bout Washintun, and didnt kno whar to go to git to stay all nite, so I stretcht my ear and skun my eye, and nuvur let on but what I were intily soun on the goos, all rite, up side up, good aag.

A fello goin by sais to anuther fello, he sais:

"D'ew you reckin he'll be at Broun's?"

The uther fello sais:

"Well, I dunno; I reckin so; Broun's is a Suthun hous, you kno."

And they went on, and I went rite arfter, gittin into Broun's hominybus, for I liked the name of Broun, it soundid so natchrul. But I didnt ixpeck thar was a man uv that commun naim in a big sitty like Washintun. It jes shows how fur from the fax uv the kais a man's idees is which spens his dais at hoam, sein only his akewaintunsis. Peepul is peepul, Billy, everywhar, and they aint much bigger nor eny better one plais than anuther; ef enything, they are wusser and littler.

Dont you think I had unother fuss about my chex, (a chek ar a roun, or squar, or dimunt shapt peece of mettil, puter sumtimes, but ginyrully brass—a brass reseat the trunk man gives you fur yo trunx when you git in the car, which you must give it back to him agin befo you kin git yo trunx,) arfter all my sufrin in

Richmun? Its the truth, Billy, ef uver I tole it; und it cum, is I sed befo, uv startin on Friday. I orto give up my chex to a man on the steembote, which clex um. I wont narrate the botherashun uv it all; but it perswadid me more and more uv the vally uv that that was inside the trunx that give me so much trubble. I sais no more at present.

Way went the hominybust goin to Broun's, hax folrin behine, and sum runnin ahed, grate nois inside, and the travelers sayin uv nuthin to I nuther, but lookin out the winders to see what they could see. Thar is housis and peepul, uv cose, but nuthin wuth menshuin untwel you git to the Smithsoniun Institeut, which it is on yo lef han is you go to Broun's. This manshin are not a gearl's skool, like the Buckingame Institeut, but what the meaning uv it is don't appear to be ginrilly understood. Fum awl I cood gether, the objic is to tend to the wether; you've heerd uv the cluk uv the wether; well, he lives in this buildin, sumwhar; it being very large nobody don't very often lay eyes on him. In regard uv its exturnels, the Institeut remines me uv a par of casters. Its culler is red, and when I has lookt at it freekwently, it looks like a hole passel uv steepils had got lost, and were kunsultin together kow to git back to the cherchis whar they belongd. But I shill have more to say on this pint in anuther letter. Onqueschinubbly, it are a strange kunsern.

When we got to Broun's, which we did pritty soon, I felt a feelin uv aw, for it wer a imments struckcher. Its length, Billy, is nearly a squar, (but you dont kno what a squar in a sitty is: I'll tell you sum these tiems,) and its about is high is you can fling a rock, bilt all uv white marvel the frunt uv it, the bak uv it bein common brik, and not so high in the ar. Inside thar wuz the same crowd and the same fuss that I told you uv at the Ixchange in Richmun, only at Broun's evrybody was a grate man.

I liked Mr. Broun. He's a small man, with sandy whiskers on his jaw, drest jam up, and very perlite. I put my name doun on his book in my best riting with pekewlyer sattisfacshin. I follerd a I'shmun up stars loaded with my trunx, ixpectin the same granjer uv marvel I had seen on the frunt uv the hous to pervale evrywhar. But I wuz disapintid cummin to my room, and struk with reel wunder and delite. Evrything wuz so intily natchrul, for a moment I didnt kno whar I wuz. "Ar this a room in Broun's marvel pallis?" I ass'd myself. "Whar is the fashunubble trundle-bed with the rollin footbode, whar the marvel-top washstan, the splendid bewro, the gold-embroydud kertins, and things?" They warnt thar, Billy. No, thank Goodniss! The bed were a good, narrer, high bed, high postid, but without any teester and vallins—jest sich a bed as the kuntry afodes most enywhar. In like manner, the washstan uv plane wood, with a little ole pitcher and bole that lookt so frenly to me, well knowin uv thar familyur patturn. The white kertin uv the winder had the ginuine Buckingame frindge, and Billy, the lookin glass were idintikly the same which par bought when he went to Richmun to see Lee Fate, the French Ginrul which fot the Revolushun with Washintun. Ef thar had bin a rag carpit, split-bottum cheers, and a fier plais, instid uv a gridi'un to burn rock cole, the thing would have bin kumpleat. As it wuz, it lookt so much like hoam, I laid doun and went to sleep befo I node it.

Nite had cum when I riz frum my slumbus. Tryin to git to the suppur table, I got out uv doors, for Broun's is a komplekatid hous with many passagis and star cases. The hac-drivers, standin

3

outside with whips in thar hans, like to took me by vilents. Nuver did I see fools mo ankshus about 1 po man they hadn't heerd uv, much mo seen, befo. They wantid to show me the fashins, but what did I keer 'bout fashins, bein uv a sighintiffick man on bisnis uv the utmus impawtents? But a carridge driver wuz alwais opinyunatid, doun to a nigger that drives a ox cart for fodder. I cussd all uv um, and went to supper up in the secund story.

Broun's dinin room aint eekul to Ballud's. It's kunsiderubly bigger, divided by foldin doors, separatin the ladis eetin room from the men's, and havin a vriety uv tabils. Powful eetin goes on here, speshly at dinner, which they gives you a akount uv, printid on a peece uv papur, named a Bill uv Far. I wanted some cole chine and turnup sallet fur supper, but coodint git enny. Uv the eeting at this tavun, which it is kopious abundant day and nite, I kin dwell on it no mo, seein how long this letter drors.

Arfter supper, I set in that part uv the hous in tween the frunt door and the plais whar you sine yo name on the book, a paved plais, havin seets uv hoss-har roun the walls, and pritty off'n okupied by peepul which assembils heer to set and do nuthin. I set thar tel midnite, reading the fisonomy uv the crowd, and formin apinyuns, which I shall deliver myself uv not now. Neether ar I going to give you my thots uv the genrul apeerunts of Washintun as I seen it nex day in the morning and for sevrul days in suckseshun. I tern to a matter uv higher impote. It ar this:

I foun that Broun charged Two Dollus and a Haf a day fur bode, with a extry charge uv Fifty Cents fur fier uv rock cole, which I had when the rain cum leeking into my charmber. Two hocksids, and three lodes uv loose tobacco, cuddent stan this long, you may be sho: wharpun I flewd aroun to fine a remmydy—in uther words, a cheeper plais, howuver much I didint like cheep doins in this pint uv vew, that it interfeerd with the dignity and impawtents uv my skeam, which you understand very well, knowing is well is I do the vally of rispectability in this life.

Akordingly, arfter exercizin grate jedgemint in s'lcktin the man fur to inquier uv in the case, I drawd nigh unto a sorter yung gentilmun which set aloan frum the kumpany, whar nobody cood hear how ignunt I was. He wuz a man of sense, evyduntly; had him a cleer, pale face, without eny beerd; and his eye wuz soft and kunsiderin—not one uv them hard, sharp eyes that is alwais lookin out like a hungry shote fur shelled corn arfter he has eet it all up. His face wuz cole as well as pale, and when he shakt me by the han, he barly techt it. You'll say this ar a bad sine, and I used to think so too. But I has ubsurved this Billy:

A hickry cole has the whitist ashes, but arfter you git throo the ashes, it's the hottest kine uv a cole—and nuthin wrops itself titer roun a thing than a snaik. Tharfo I dont put no overwhelmin confidents in these heer warm fellers that shakes you so harty by the han, wroppin thar fingers tite and holdin you longer than you want to be hilt, and tellin you affecksnitly how glad and all they is to see you.

Well, it turned out igzackly is I ixpected. This gentilmun, which I has sense becum well akwainted with him, arfter listining indiffrintly to my condishin, and lookin at me very camly, took a intrust in me, and helpt me cleen throo to whar I am at this momint.

His name wuz Mr. Argruff, and he cums to see me and I go to see him. He's a frenly man, certin.

Me and Mr. Argruff wuz two dais goin roun to the bodin housis; I recken we went to a hundud.  But he dident goe with me to the fust one, becos I, bein like evrybody else, wuz afeerd to let out all at wunst how I warnt abil, for the presint, to pay fur a rispecktable plais, sich as my projick demandid, and, arfter a while, will onquestchunubbly bring.  So I went by myself to a hous he pinted out to me, and when I seen the lanlady (the desentist I has yet seen), she curtchid perlitely, and I inquired, techin my hat, fur a room.  She sais:

"Are you a member, ser?"

I reflected a minit, and then anserd,

"Yes'm, O! yes'm."

She lookt at me rite good, and then she shode me a apartmint not much bigger'n a tater hole, nisely furnisht to be sho, but barly big nuff to turn roun in.  I tole her I were a sizibul man, which liked elbo room.  She lookt at me agin.

"Whut Stait ar you from?" she sais.

"Ole Ferginny, mum."

She lookt at me agin, harder'n ever.  Then she took me to anuther cumpartmint, uv far size, but planely furnisht as to bed, carpit, etsetry.  It wer pritty dark in thar, and a few chunks uv wood, the fust I had seen, was smouldrin on the hath.  She shet the door.  I felt commykill, but I see the room was lit by a winder in the sealin, called a sky-lite.  She sais, talkin rapidly, like wimmen most in ginrully do:

"This is a very nise room, one of the most kumfutable in the hous, and so conveenyunt, and yit out uv the way like.  Guvner Jones staid here all las' sesshin, sayin it was a charmin room; and Jedge Forney, he had it fur three years; jest arfter Ginrul Scott and the Forrin Ministers and thar ladies got rooms with me. Oh! we alwais have plescnt kumpny, and my boders, bein pleesed, don't leeve me, but this is the fust of the sesshin like, which is the reesin I have a few spar rooms, but only a very few. The room aint cleaned up this mornin, our maid was taken sick lass nite, but its a fine room, the ferniteur is not igzackly new, which soots a singul gentilmun that doant like to feel crampt. Here's yo tabil, and ef you rite much, the lite falls straight down on yo papur. This winder, openin into the Cote" (here she histed a winder I thought warnt thar at all), "gives you cool ar all day long, speshilly in summer. I know you'l like to set at this winder and choo tubacker, which is the habit of all Ferginny gentilmen, and thar is a fine wall you kin spit aginst."

Imagin, Billy, a squar inside uv a icehous, verry deep, bilt up uv brik, and a winder cut in the extreem bottom, lookin into the inside uv it, and you'l have some idee uv this winder, and the 4 walls uv a high hous runnin up around it. I sertny like to set at a up star's winder, in my cote off, uv a summur day, and spit ambeer aginst the neck uv a chimbly, but I dont admier a room with a winder openin out upon nuthin but darkness and brix.

So we coodent agree about nether uv them rooms, altho one had a fine wall to spit aginst, and so we went up a flite uv steps to look at anuther room. You know she had very few to spar. Well, this was a reel splendid room, but she assed too much munny fer it, and then we lookt at three or four mo, but all wuz too high priced. All the tiem I wuz lookin at rooms, she wur lookin at me in a way that made me feel very cuyus, fur I had heerd that evrybody in Washintun, wimmin and all, wuz mighty cute, and I thought I seen she knew what I cum fer. It's alwais

the way with enybody that's got a secrit. How cood she know
what I was arfter? The thing were ixsplained when I went to
go. She diden git mad becos I dident bode with her, but jest as
I was leavin she sais,

"Ixcuse me, ser, but didden you say you wuz a member?"

When she had fust made this inquiry, I diden kno what she
ment, and I diden kno now, but I wuz bleest to stand up to what
I had sed, so I sais agin,—

"Yes'm, Oh, yes'm."

"From Ferginny?"

"Sertny, mum."

"What deestric."

Then it flasht upun me, and you may depen' upon it, I felt like
a fool. But I upt and tole her the plain fac. I tole her I had
mistook her meanin entily, that I warnt no member uv Kongriss,
but what I ment wuz, I wuz a member uv serciety.

She lafft so good nachud, I felt sorry I cudent aford to stay
thar and spit on her wall. When I went back to Broun's, and
had foun Mr. Argruff, (he don't bode thar,) I tole him about it,
he lafft, and sed he must go out with me and help me out. So he
done. We went, and we went, and went, untel we found a plais
that he said wuz the plais fur me, which is the plais I'm now
ritin in.

¶ Two days we wuz at it, and Billy, the Lord knows, (as yonr
par sais,) I diden beleeve the sivilized wirld cuntained the derty
housis, and derty, po, miserbul, retchid, slip-shod, draggledy,
har-uncombed wimmen that I seen them two dais. Sum uv um
look so pityful, and sum so meen and feerce; and skeersly one
uv um was drest desunt. I swar I felt sorry for the sitty of Wash-

intun; but then agin the ladies in the street appear to have mity
nice close, and sum uv um magniffysent. How to account fur
this, I dont know. Washintun is a onakountabul plais, men is
well is wimmin. ‖

All uv um wantid me to bode át thar housis, and all offud me
such indusements that I wood have takin at the droppin uv a hat,
but for Mr. Argruff sayin no. One po, kine-harted cretur a'most
begd me to take a garrit room at her bous, reckumendin it hily.

"It's a sweet, little room," she sais, "retide, and havin a good
vew uv the Avnew," (that's the main street in Washintun,) "and
you won't bump yo hed in it. Thar is no fier-plais, but its rite
warm ixcep in extreem cole wether, and you need'nt bump yo
hed ef you be keerful to stoop. It's nisely furnisht, and the sealin
slopes a leetle, but you won't bump yo hed in the middle uv the
room, and you are rite tall too."

The po cretur seemed to think all wuz rite ef I diden bump
my hed. I expec hern has been bumpt, and she is techt in the
brane. Anuther reckmendid her attentive maids, anuther her
nigger boy, anuther this, and anuther that. All had some grate
men livin with um, and all lookt as if they suffered much frum
sumthin or nuther. I inclien to the apinyun that many uv um
drinks. They tell me the hole toun uv Washintun is a bodin
hous, and that the po wimmen that keeps boders is increesin rap-
pidly every year, and with thar increese thar is a increese uv
misry, you may rest ashode. In fac, a bodin hous keepin womun
is a sine bode of misry, nothin mo, igsept in a few kases.

When finely I got to whar I'm now, I sed to Argruff, it were
hard work to git sootid. Yes, he said, but I had a eesyer time
and better luck than most peepul that come to this sitty to sojern,

and I reckin maybe he's rite.   I stop here, sendin my luv to all inquirin frens, and keepin in resurve a thousand things fur my next.   Good bi, Billy.

From yo faithful fren,

MOZIS ADDUMS.

## THIRD LETTER.

MR. ADDUMS DESCRIBES HIS FELLO-BODERS AND SEES AND
HEERS THINGS.

DEAR BILLY:

/| Washintun, in ginrul, inside or out, ar sertny a
quare toun. Out uv the hous, things is very scattrin and diffykilt
uv komprenshin, lookin, as it twuz, like a man had gethered together the mateyul uv a sitty, and, being drawd off frum his bizniss, had gone sum whar to aten to anuther contrac, leevin things
layin about loose, intendin to retern and jine 'um up bimeby. Its
jest like a feel uv wheet, that has been sowed by a drunkin fool
uv a nigger; here the patchis is too thick, and thar thar is skeersly
a blade. The streets is prodigeous brawd, givin plenty uv elbo
room for evrything to tun aroun, which is a good thing, thar bein
so many hax and other veekles uv all kines. The beet uv hax
espeshily, I has nuver kunseeved. Eny man goin by i uv the
principil tavuns, sich is Broun's, the Gnashnul, or Willuds, and
seein the hax stretcht out in a string thar, wood swar his sacrid
affydavid that a feunrul wuz goin to come outin thar immejitly.
But they is jest waitin to take passingus, it bein sich a long ways
frum eny whar to eny whar. Nobody that hasint got good kuntry legs, like mine, with plenty uv caf, and used to hunting skwer-
rils all day and chasin ole hars when a boy, kin stan to go frum

ɪ plais to anuther.    But I kin stan it, good, and saves a good eel
uv munny tharby, nuver takin a hack which kosts you a quorter
or a haf, or imployin uv a homnybust, which only chargis 4punts.ɪ(
Inside the hous, things in Washintun is jest as kramd is they is
loose outside.    Ether this ar the case, or Mr. Argruff, in selektin
my bodin hous, had a eye to makin uv me a stewjint uv men and
mannus.    Billy, you've no idee how peepil is packt in little housis
like the wun I'm okkypine.    Packin uv poke in a meat hous,
which you shood be keerful it don't git het at the bone, and prizin
uv tobarker, which y'all's Winstun knows how to do it, givs you
a parshil idee, but only parshil.    Now, in the fust place, in this
hous, which I'm a bodin in it, thar is a sto for the sellin of men's
shirts, limbur-twig appels and mint-stick kandy and doll-babis.
Then thar is anuther sto of mancher-makin, wimmin's kotes and
klose and things, and that is all the reglur bizness done heer, at
leest all I has yit found out. ixsept ɪ thing which it do puzzil me
mitey ni too deth.    And that ar this : Lookin out uv my back winder, which ar the onliest winder I've got, thar is anuther winder jinin
it to the lef, and lookin thoo that winder I sees rite into a loft, and
thar I'll be konsoun if thar aint a sine bode uv a tavun with a star
on it, and ferther on a lite comin in from sum whar, like the lite
over the top uv a fashnuble door, and what the meenin uv it is is
mo'n I kno, or kin konjecktcher.    I've set for hows and hows,
waitin for somebody to cum into that tavun through that ar fur
door, and nar a soul has enturd it yit, unlest while I wuz asleep.
But if eny body uver does cum thar, I lay I ketch um.
To retern to my akount.    Besides the two stos I abuv menshind, and the misteyus sine bode uv the tavun, thar is mo peepul
bodin in this hous than you kin shaik a stic at, and I dont reckin

I've seen evin haf uv um eether, long as I has been heer. Uv them I seen, the fust ar, uv koas, a Kongrismun, coz evry hous must have a Kongrissmun, which ginrully takes the bess room in the hous, two uv um in fac. Our Kongrismun is name Honner-bul Mister Swomplans, but whar he's frum, I hasn't a idee, only I kno he's a mitey smart man and reeds so meny books that his two rooms can't hole all uv um, so he's bleest to fill the passagis and star-casis, leevin barly room for peepil to pass. What wood-ent I give to have his sense. I has nuver seen him good, but he's ruther ole, and a good many foax cums to see him. I think they calls him Guvner; evry Kongrissmun bein naterully a Guvner, a Ginrul or a Kunel.

Arfter Guvner Swomplans cums anuther ole man, which his name is Jedge Foskit (evrybody in this toun that aint a Kon-grismun and has reecht a mejum age, bein a Jedge) and he's a man of biznes in the lor, and has got him a clame agin the Guv-vermint, which is mostly the kais with all them in Washintun which aint got no reglur offis. Jedge Foskit is a pow'ful profane man, coz I heer him cussin his washwomun, coz he can't pay her. This looks strange to me too, for the reesin that he's got gray har and a gole hedid kane, lookin so dignyfide throo his gole specktickles, like a good ole man that blongs to the Cherch, and luvs to do favers to peepul. But thar is wun thing about him I don't like, and that ar his nose, which the eend uv it igzackly re-sembils a oke ball, sich as we boys used to make red ink out uv at ole feel skool. I kno he takes his dram freely, and its a pitty his claim agin the Guvvermint aint fur licker—he'd git it certin.

Then thar is wun mo ole man knectid with the Post-Offis and the railrode. I'v heerd him talkin loud and harty freekwintly, but dont kno him when I see him, becoz I nuver has seen him, it bein so dark up stars heer.    Livin in a leetle bit uv a room rite by this ole railroad man, is I dont kno how meny'yung Ishmen, that cums in way in the nite and gets up soon in the morning without sayin a wird.    Then agin rite over my bed is sum dutch-germuns, the saim what has the mancher-makin sto I tole you uv, and wun nite I woke up puffickly wild frum a dreem and the noise going on abuv me; and what do you reckin it all wuz, Billy?    Blamed ef too littil dutch-germun childun wåsn't born almost rite on top uv me.    I jess tell you, a thing of this sort are praps the most terryfine thing on erth.    Consoun the creturs! they cries a heep, and I think a dutch-germun baby cries more savitch than any uther, keeping you awake, and frettin you, and disposin you agin matrymuny.

Besides all these, thar is a reel ole, ole womun that rooms way up yonder sumwhar, and cums creepin doun stars, not making a nois, and skeerin me evry day like thundur.    Then thar is a room for the man and his wife, which sells the shirts and candy, and thar childun, a boy being all thar family.

But thar is mo yit.    Thar is a Mr. Oans, a yung man, a Cluk (all the yung men heer is Cluks, and a good meny ole men ix-çept sich as drives hax and sells oshters), a handsum fello, with a high forrud and pritty har on his hed, which he greezis it too much, it bein the fashun in toun.    He dont apeer to have no mitey good opinyun uv enything in this werld, and goes about and looks like a man which has repented uv bein born, but, bein proud, dident intend to apolygyze fer it.    He's a genrus fello, and eets mo oshters uv a nite than eny five men in the sitty, and al-wais wants me too eet with him, which I genrilly duz, not likin to hert his feelins. His room jines mine, and the very day I got heer (Mr. Argruff tellin him I was from Ferginny) he cum in and made me a presint uv a reel Woodall pipe, a good reed stem, and a hole chanse uv splendid Linchbug tubarker to smoak. I'm bleest to like him, and sense I got to smoakin his presint, it's felt a heap mo like hoam to me. Thar is redeemin pints about Washintun.

This heer Mr. Oans has got him a fren—a little ole dried up yung man uv a spishus coprus culler, which his name is Mr. Melloo, and he rites letters fur the newspapus, called corrispondunce, and this ar wun of the biggest biznesses in toun, ef I aint deseevd, which most likely I ar, fur the foax in Washinutun ar very fond uv lying on all subjicks. Mr. Melloo, he rooms heer too, makin uv no fuss and behavin jest like he wuz white, but lookin pryinly at me, whenuver he gits a chanse, percisely like wun these heer inkwisytiv little tan-culled beegles. I wondur ef he suspishuns ennything? Consoun his sole! he'd better tend to his oan biznis and let me alone. I got nuthin to do with him and dont want nuthin.

So you see, Billy, this house ar pritty well stufft with specimins uv vayus peepul. And howdyou reckin I cum to kno so much about um? Why, the gearl that wates on my room, she tole me, She's white as eny lady, speeks Ishmun langride and cums frum thar, and Billy she's plegg-taked handsum. Duz mo work, is helthier, smarter, fuller of good yumur, and better lookin than eny body I seen yit. Her name is Mayan, and I and her has a talk evry day. This elustraits the diffrents between Nothun and Sothun peepul, havin white maids heer, tho thar's a good chanse uv niggers too, while we all has cullud maids, likely mlatters, freakwently.

Fur the furst few days I wer so shamed to see this pritty gearl fixin up my bed and histin cole on my stove, I coodent speek, and when I did speek (askin how to git in at nite, when the door was shet on the strete) she seen frum my tremblin vois and gentmuny mannur that I thought I wuz talkin to a reel lady, and sense then she's got a great fantsy to me.  She's got blak har (wavin), blak eyes, that is brite and quick-movin as litenin, and *smart?* I jes tell you, she's a reglar Spanish needle of a gearl.  You git to foolin arfter her, like Mr. Oans and Melloo, ptickly Oans, which is alwais trying to outdo her in sayin smart things—and I be bound you think you've ketcht a razur by the blaid instid uv the handil.  I think it wer Chusdy mornin I heerd Mr. Oans sayin to her—he's very fond uv asking her knundrums and speakin broag like they do in her kuntry.  He sais:

"Well now, Marry," he sais, "will you tell me won thing?"

"Shure," she sais, "I'm glad yure afther increesin yure infermashin.  What's it, Misther Oans?"

"Well," he sais, "ken you tell me who wuz the father of Zebby dee's childer?"

"The father of Zebby dee's childer?" she sais.  "Faith, I don't wonder you're askin.  I think he was a ghentilmun"—meanin by this, Billy, that Mr. Oans want akwaintid with no gentilmen.

But this aint nuthen to what she sais sumtimes; I wisht I cood remember her sayins, but they is so keen you can't ketch holt uv um even with yo mine.  In the week days, when she's cleenin up the rooms—she attends to the hole hous—uv koas she cant look very nise, but you jes orto see her drest up uv a Sundy.  By

jings! it duz me good, yes, good, to look at her. And plegg take
her! she knows it. Dernd ef ole Mr. Kongismun Swomplans
dont watch her reglar throo his winder as she goes up the strete
to the Kathlick Cherch. He's rite, too; Oans and Melloo duz
the saim thing, and goes long to church with her sum times at
nite. This 'll kinder strike you as goin too fur, but peepul duz
jes is they plees in Washintun, and nobody dont keer nuthin fur
nobody nor nuthin.

Mayan she sleeps up stars with that ar ole woman, and it ar a
cuyus fac, Billy, that wun uv these heer tarryfine ole wimmin is
kep in evry bodin hous in Washintun. They tries to hide um, so
that fellers cummin to git rooms cant see um, but the miserbul, po
creturs kin alwais tell when enybody is a lookin aroun, and will
poke thar ole skeer-faces out uv sum hole or ruther.

I'm a givin you a long akount uv all thes peepul in oddur to
give you a idee uv the way things is dun heer and the kind uv
foax that lives in the sitty. Now skeersly nun uv we all eets at
this heer hous whar we sleep, but gits our meels at anuther hous,
cunsernin which I'm a goin to tell you in my nex letter. Less
change the subjick.

When I fust got heer, Injuns was all the go—Por-knees, Soos,
Potty-wotty-mees, Socks and Focksis, and I dunno how menny
mo, about 20 or 30 in number, all drest up in red blankits, fethers,
paintid faces, rings in thar ears, bar's claws, mokkysins, tommy-
hawks, and so forth and setry—reel Injuns, Billy. I dun seen um
till I'm tide, and they dont intruss me no mo. Jeemony! how
yaller and ugly they is, and how the ladies duz luv to look at um
and shake thar hands! You needent tell me bout they being
Aboridgyknees, and the lost Ten Tribes uv Jeus, spoke uv in the

Bibil. They is nuthin in the wirld but mlatters which run way from thar marsters a long time ago, and dun run wild like hogs in a mounten. That's what they is, and you cant fool me, and make me bleeve yo fantsyful storis 'bout um. No sir-ree, I used to think they wuz red like boys that paintid thar fase with poak-berries, but they aint, they is yaller mlatters, and nuthing else. ṗ

Nex to the Injuns, it cum nachrul fur me to pay my rispecks to the public bildins, which thar is a grate meny uv, bilt most in ginrully uv marvel, and wood be a site to see ef you cood cum acrost um suddinly in a piney wood, like that betwixt Passin Merrydith's and Ganwy's Mill, but heer is very commun indeed and nuthin out'n the way. Is I sed before, nun uv um aint finisht, not even the Captul, and pun top uv nearly all uv um thar is things sumthin like the big king-post to a sale vessil, only bigger, but mo like the figger 4 trigger to a imments partrich trap, only wun peese are a roap instid uv wood. But the bildins aint traps that I kno uv, ixcept to ketch munny, and these heer big triggers is intendid to hiest rock. You've seen the like on a railrode; thar wuz wun at Buffalo Bridge, this side uv Fomvil. It ar custumerry fur strangers to go first to the Patint Offis, which I went along, uv koas, and seen sites I tell you—two or three milyuns uv curosties frum all parts uv the gloab, and a heap, mo moddils uv masheens, all in glass casis. Berds and beests, munkis and snaiks, rocks and figgers, and pictchers, and everything, doun to ole Genrul Washintun's solgir close, and skreech owils and aags. Ded peepul too, and heds cut off, and humin bones, horryfine to behole.

The mornin I wer up thar, Mr. Oans he wer thar, and I warnt akwaintid with him then, but follerd'long behine, apeerintly 'thout intendin it, becaze he wuz with some ladies and what they all sed

ixplained things to me. Peard like the ladies, wun uv um, wuz
mitey smart and yumrus, laffin and makin Mr. Oans laff, in his
dont keer way at what she sed.   I coodint begin to tell you wun
haf uv it all, but wun thing I wer bleest to remember, it struck me
so foasbly.   Goin roun wun uv the glass casis, she remarkt—

"Law! Mr. Oans, do cum heer, and look at this."

He went roun, and I heerd him inquier.   He says:

"Well, what is it?"

She sais, talkin like a little chile, jes lernin:

"Why," she sais, "jes look doun thair at them mair's aags—
ain't they mair's aags?"

"Ashoridly," he sais, "and ef you wuz to tern wun uv um
over, it wood be a colt's revolver."

Then they all bust out a laffin predidgus, but I dident see no
sense in it.   Presinly they went on, and I went roun and lookt.
Sho nuf, it wer a aag big nuf to be a mar's aag, (a hoss mar, I
meen,) but I don't bleeve wun word uv it.   I nuver seen no mar
settin on no ness hatchin no colts, and you nuther.

They all walkt on into the masheen room, whar they didint
stay long, but lef me thar lookin at the wheals, and spokes, and
jigamarigs untwell my hed farly whirld.   Arfter keerful igsami-
nashin, I coodint say I thought much uv eny uv thease inven-
shins, which posbly sum uv may be very good—fur the present.   I went away frum thar, but go thar okashunly when I git
loansome, which Mr. Oans he sais a pawnbroker (whatuver that
is,) is very apt to be loansome.

All this tiem you may be certin I wer keepin a sharp look out
fur my biznis.   Wun tiem, I had a grate mine to tell Mr. Argruff
'bout it, but arfter reflecktin tho't I'd better say nuthen too soon.

Nether have I mehshind enything to eny uv our Ferginy Kongrismun, which I've bin interjuiced to, Mr. Letchur, Mr. Bocox frum
our deestric, Mr. Powl, Mr. Edmund's sun, Mr. Clemmings, Jedge
Casky, and them; all wise, kine hartid gentilmen, willin to do eny
thing fur you they ken.   Sum uv um I got akwaintid with befo I
lef Broun's tavun, wun day when I wer takin sperits, pritty good,
too, heep bettern that at the Junkshin, with Mr. Argruff.   They
jined very perlitely, and, heerin whar I wer frum, commenst on
pollytix, askin how I stood.   You know how a good drink takes
the bashful out uv a feller, so I talked rite up to them grate Kongrismun jes like I wood to peepil born and raisd at crost rodes.
I tole um I wer a outenout, ole fashin, strait up and doun, Staits
rite, Jacksin, Kansis dimmokrat, bleevin in nuthin but what the
party bleevd in, votin fur a dimmokrat aginst eny body, I don't
keer hoo.

"That's rite," they sais, "you stick to that, and dont trus' too
much to yo oan idees, and you'll alwais be rite."

I sais, "I thank you," and we all mendid our drinks, and I
want nigh as bashful as I wer at fust.   So I assd um a questchun
which had bothered me mitely, soon arfter I got to Washintun
whar evry body talks pollytix and you's bleeged to heer mo or
less uv what they talk about.   I sais:

"Gentilmen, sense I cum heer, evry body a'most is acusin uv
evry body uv bein uv a dimmy gog ; what ar a dimmy gog, ar it
a kind uv dimmokrat or a vessil that holes licker?"

This apeerd to amews um mitely, and wun sed, laffin, that my
urror wur very common, becoz it aint evry man which knows the
diffrens between a dimmy gog and a dimmokrat.

He sais, speakin to me, S'e, "The true diffrents is very simple, and kin be ixplained in a breth. ‖ Whoever gits electid is a dimmy gog, and whoever gits defeatid is a paytriot. D'you unnderstan?"

I told him "sertny," but, I sais, "I've heerd these heer dimmy gogs abused so much, and Gnashnul dimmokrats abused so much, that I begun to think thcy wuz the same thing idintikilly.

"Oh no!" he sais, "you must by no meens entertane sech apinyun. The Gnashnal Dimmockracy, altho they've bin electid and hold the powur uv guvunmint, ar not dimmy gogs; they ar ixcepshins to the genril rool; they ar the grate party, and however troo it may be that the party is sumwhut dividid Noth and South yet ar they inknucksorubbly conjined together by this very divishin, and stronger than they wood be without it."

I had to studdy over this some tiem befo I cood unnerstan how a thing cood be jined by a divishin. At lass I sais:

"I think I see thoo your observashin. The Gnashnul Dimmockracy of the Noth and South ar jined together like the rooms in a jale—by a thick, unpassibul rock wall betwixt um. Uv koas the jale ar stronger fur the wall."

"Ixackly," he sais, "you've hit the nale right on the hed."

I⁀I sais, "Well, I'm prowd uv sich a strong party," and so I am, Billy, and you too.

He sais, "Well you may be, fur it's the only party that kin save the Yuneyun, and that's its bizniss."

"Yes," I sais, "and it remines me powfully uv a song I reckin .. all uv you gentilmen have heerd befo now—a nigger song, but full uv meenin, calld,

> 'Ef you have eny goodin thing,
> Save it, save it;
> Ef you have eny goodin thing,
> Save *me* sum.'"

They all walkt off up stars in a roar uv larfter. I reckin I'm a gittin to be a rite funny man, or probly they laff at me becoz they think I'm a fool. I dunno.

I intended in this letter to uv tole you about my fust visit to Kongris, but kinnot.

Give my luv to Patsy Allin, yo sister Betsy and Fanny and all.

Yo fren and cussin,

MOZIS ADDUMS.

## FOURTH LETTER.

THE MINTZPI HOUSE—A KONVERSASHIN—MR. ADDUMS VISITS
KONGRIS.

DEAR BILLY:

|| We all, that is me and Oans and Melloo and Mr.
Argruff, bodes at the Mintzpi Hous, which the pies thar aint
made uv the kommin mint, but, jedgin fum thar taest, uv peppur-
mint, with a leetil injun tunups and a frakshin uv dekade colluds.
They has um evry day, regly. My idee uv a pi, ar appil dump-
lin. Potpi aint bad, pervidin you dont have no surplus uv hog
fat and bacin rines, sich as yo ant Polly ar invayubly bound to
hav. Pankakes with good thik, blak, Alleendz mlassis, is splendid.

In regards uv the other eetin thar at the Mintzpi Hous, 'taint
much. Not a crum uv konbred I've techt senst heer I've bin.
They brings to the tabil a kind uv battur-bred, which it ar certny
ar spuyus. Billy, if you cood send me a good hot pone with ole-
fashin cruss, hard is a rock, which it eets and looks like a peece
uv brokin skillit, givin uv a man's jor-teeth sum rashnul and hole-
sum exursize, you'd do me a faver. ||Ef you had a Kongrismun
thar to frank it, you cood jess rop it up in a newspapir and send
it rite along. Franking ar a Kongrismun ritin uv his name on
eny thing, which it then goes free in the Postoffis all over krea-

shin. I wondir when the Kongrismun gits on the car they dont
rite thar naim on thar oan bax, and go gratis. But you see guvunmint is sich a fool it pays um fur cummin, callin uv it mielidge.
Billy, spose you wuz to hi a man to do sum dichin, and wuz to
pay him a hevy price fur doin uv it: woodint you think he were
distracktid ef he wuz to ass you to pay him extry fur cumin to
whar he cood git to his wuk? Uv koas. When I lived ovsee
fur Doctellick Dillin, I walkt ten miel in the rain to git thar, and
the idee of chargin him nuthin fur goin thar nuver entud my hed.
I'd a thot I wuz a fool ef it had. But sich is Kongris. Oans
tells me thar's a Senytur here in Washintun that has bilt him a
puffick pallis with wun trip uv mile money. And a member from
Jorjy hav bilt him a whole toun with the saim, which for the reesin he calls it Mileidgvil.

At the Mintzpi, which Oans—he's a funne fello, he calls it the
Mintpizin Hous, sayin he bleeves they seezins the pize thar with
assnick—thar's a whole chanse of boders, a heep uv um ladies,
old and yung, pritty and ugly, prinsipilly hoamly, marrid and
singil. I tell you they dressis outin the ashis. Caliker? I aint
sean a stich, I aint smelt caliker wunst over thar. They doant
mine nuthin. Arms bar up to the arm pits, necks nakid, free as
ar. Ded uv winter, too: sno on the groun, thurmonitur doun to
zeeroe. By jing! I wondir what wimmin's skins is maid uv.
I'me be dad shimd ef they wuz jes tanned ef they woodint maik
the warmist kine uv shoo that uver wuz wo. Kin cole pennytrait
um? It kin sertny not. Then agin these heer ladies, drest so
nise, is monsus keerful uv thar close, histin thar kotes hi and fer
up in wet wether, not shamed nor feard of nobody.

A number, in fac most uv these ladis I dunno; a few I duz; mo ptickly Miz Hanscum, which her husbun he's gone to Kallyforny, and Miss Saludy Trungil, which she's a very grait frend uv Oans and Melloo, and Mr. Argruff okashinully ingagis her in konversashin late at nite. Miz Hanscum she's powful pritty, powful, and so eesy to git akwainted with, being afecshinit I jedge. They say she's mitey ritch, and I reckin its so, fur she wars a site uv joolry uv the finest kine. Miss Saludy Trungil, she's a remarkably stylish looking gearl, bein tall, handsum formd, full uv sense, and a leetil sassy I ixpec. She and Oans is mitey thick. Mr. Argruff, he injoyze her, and even this heer kuyus, punkin-facetid littil Melloo, he grins orful at her sumtiems. She's boun to be smart. At a nuther tiem I shill tell you how I cum to know thees ladis.

⑴ Uv koas thar's a large passil uv gentilmen at the Mintzpi—Senytuz, Ripryzentativs, Ginruls, Jedgis, Clux, and so foth, with thar wievs and dorters, tho' the clux they cant afode to hav no wievs, being retchid po they tell me. Billy, it ar wuth a man's while, which has bin used to commun plantashin life, to cum in heer to thees tremenjus tavun bildins, with their marvil flores, splendid parlus, and bewtiful carpits, to see the fine foax, and speshilly the ladis, sailin long the passagis heer and at Brouns, and the Gnashnul and Willud's. They rarr back so proud! They has sich hoops; they go by you so skonful; and the soun uv thar silks and satins skrapes yo very nurves, makin uv the skin uv yo body krorl and yo ize uv yo hed to git dark with a swimmy-fine mist at the site of so much magniffysent frock surroundin wun littil woman, which you cant bleeve she blongs to the famly of Adum and Eave, born to sin and sorro.⑴ No Billy, thees proud cretus is lifted high abuv mawtality, and seein uv um, you stans thar cole in your goose-skin, afflicted with a abomminable cents uv infeyorrity. Jes fur the saik uv the ixsperymint, you feel like you'd like to taik wun uv thees gloyus beans into a pees uv ploud groun and pull a fishin worrum out uv whar its jess been turnd over by the mole bode and put it rite into the pam of her littil white han. You warnt to cumpar what's in her han with the han itself, and then flosfize upon the subjict.

Me and Oans and Melloo was talkin 'bout this heer very thing the uther nite in Oan's room, and Mr. Argruff he cum in while we wuz kunversin and evury wunst in a whiel techin sum uv the finist kine uv Robsin County, Tennysy, whiskey, which Hon. Mr· Joans he give to Oans. I remarked pritty much what I has giv you abuv, and Oans, (which ar the kuyusist yung man in the wirld,) Oans he sais " Mozis," we's very familyar now, " Mozis," he sais, "you do great injestis to the far secks uv Washintun sitty. Soe far frum not likin fishin worrums, thay ar very fond uv um. Don't you know that thay taiks um and bleechis um and cooks um and eets um?"

"Shuh!" I sais, "you cant fool me."

S'e "Its a fac, I asho yon. Thay jes cuts off the eens uv um and eets um. Thay ar wun of the mos' fashnubble dishes uv polisht suckles, and the Frentch naim fur um is mackaroney."

I lookt at him, and seen his kountinunts were intily cumposed. Then I wundud at the humin nacher of fine dresst wimmin in sittis that eets fishin worrums and call um by the naim that Yankee Doodil called his poney. And I has sens lernt that fashnubbil peepul eats musheroons, esteamin uv um uv a grate delikissy.

Littil, ole Melloo ar a cole bloodid po' cretur, and when he sets in a rume straddils rite roun a stoav, like it wuz a littil nigger boy he wuz drawin in 'tween his legs to pat him on the hed. He dont say so mitey much, and akordin what he duz say souns mo'n what it is, caws its rar. He spoak up.

S'e "The Buckingame man (me, you kno, Billy,) ar rite. All wimmin are dirt. The identitty's absloot. I shood like to see Addumsis ixperrymint tride. Dirts vary. Sum's good and sum's bad, sum's wirth cultervaytin and sum aint. And I reckin Addums can tell us what the farmus put in dirt to improve it."

S'I "Menyo, gorno."

S'e "Igzactly. The sitty sivlizashun uv wimmin is but the adawnment uv so mutch oridginal femail mud with a cantankerus crop uv silks and ribbins foaced up by the stimulus uv gold, the only troo soshul and plitykul gorno."

"Cum," sais Mr. Argruff, "this ar very wrong talk for men that has mothers and sisters. None uv you bleeve a wird you say. Mozis here is very yung"—

"Well," I sais, "I'm tolibul yung both in ears and ixspeyunts, but I'm 20 and considerbul upuds."

"Well," s'e "when you git to be is ole is I am, you'll be mo charytuble. Thees yung ladis ar vane. But evrybody is vane"—

"Yes," I sais, "all is vanyty seth the preechur."

"Peepil maik a distinkshin," he kontinyud, not mindin me, "between vanyty and pride, praisin wun and pretendin to dispics the uther. It's troo, fur mettyfisicul pupposis, they kin he sepratid, but, in pint of fac, they are wun and the saim thing—the saim impults actin in diffrint dreckshins Konshus powur; that's it. Ejeckt it apun the boddy, it is vannyty; infews it into the sperit, it's pride. Bewty is womun's power; yes, and man's too. Pride is sed to be the basis of ambishun, and ambishun the movin foase

5

uv the soldjer and the staitsmun. But you nuver saw a grate woryur or emnent staitsmun who wasn't at hart a thousan tiems mo vane then the vanist gearl that sweeps the floes uv Broun's parlers as tho she wuz Klepatry, and had Seezur and Antny and Roam and Ejipp, eye ! the hole wirl at her feet."

"Good !" says Oans.

"Robsin Kounty whisky," says Melloo,

Mr. Argruff, he went on, sayin uv :

"And Mozis complanes uv thar skon. But skon is nuthin but a nuther naim for ignorunts, which indeed ar the jenerick turm for awl humin foltz. Wimmen and men only skon thoes hoom they doant kno, or hoom they reely kunsider unwirthy.

"Thar is wimmin at Broun's and the Gnashnul and the Mintzpi, hoo think so meenly uv me that my presintz maiks no impreshin on thar auguns uv vishin—they can't possibly see me. But neethur the man nor the womun ever breatht the breth of life hoo cood skon me after wunst I huv walkt camly up to the dores uv thar soles and knockt. And I'll wajur that the proudist lady in Washintun will luv Mozis Addums arftur she cums to know him. Wimmen fantsy wild fellers, but they ar compeld by a lor uv thar nachur to *luv* sich men as Mozis. In all thar silk and jooils they wood be glad to see him in his hoamspun close ; thar harts spontainyusly goes out to meet an honest, simple-minded, onsuspishus cretur like him."

" But," I sez, " I ar suspishus—spishus is the devil, and I've got good close is enybody in my trunk, but I'm not a gointer war um evry day. Then agin flatrin a man to his fais is bad mannus, I didn't keer how well twuz ment."

" Well, we wont quorl about that," he sais. " I beg yo pardin.

But you do our Washinton gearls injestis. Didgever go with the gearls on a fishin frolick, Mozis? "

"Imfatkly, I has," I sais.

S'e "wuzint it plesint?"

"It were prime," I sais.

S'e "No dout. And you fown yo gearls wuz jest is pritty and sweete way off in the woods and by the waters is they wuz at hoam in the drawin room. Its jes so with thees gearls heer. Taik um out in the kuntry and you'll fine they ar is natchrul thar is a tree or a blaid uv grass. The fac is, Mozis, a gearl is like a sac cote; she fits eny body, or ruther I shood say any plais."

Then he stopt, and sighd, and kep silent.

"Go on," sais Oans.

I sais the saim.

Melloo, handin doun the bottil uv Tennysy whisky sais, "taik a littil sperits."

Mr. Argruff filld him up a squerril lode and rezumed.

S'e "I'm a retchid man—a retchid man. And all becoz uv a dreem which I had it fotty senturis ago, and has ever sintz bin trine to realize it. In vane! I've but wun wish in this life, and my prar is this: Sum sweet, bloo summer day, the sweetist that ever dornd, I wish to spend aloan under the trees and by the worters with the most bewtiful wumum in the wirl. We must be abslootly aloan, and we must be togethur all day, frum the risin uv the sun to the goin doun uv the saim."

"What!" says Oans, "without eny thing to eet? Fo' fride ("meenin oshters, you kno Billy) by all meens—fo' apeece."

"No," I sais, "sum fride chickin, buttud biskits, and a fishin line."

Mr. Argruff, he went on like he nuver heerd nun uv us. "While the lite lasts, let me look deep into the hevin uv her ize and listen to the music uv her vois. When the day trimbles in deth, and when the sun sens his last red shaft from the purpal hills, let me press my lips to her oan, and let that last sunray be a javlin uv fier to kunsome me thar, utt'ly, so that I shall becum so mutch blank spais; fer ef evin wun pottikil uv my mateyul body remaned, the memry uv that day uv blis wood revivvyfy and ixpand it into a senchent sole, kapebil uv the pane uv longin fer that whitch it cood cum agin no mo frevver, or ef it kaim, wood not be whut ferst it wuz."

Oans seemed techt, and sed he'd had that idee ofting. Little ole Melloo sais very sarkastick, "Argruff, lemme advies you to set up a retale poitry shop. Git a masheen, and werk it with Rob'sin County Whisky."

I says, "Mr. Argruff, did you think you wuz marrid to that ar gearl?"

"No," he sais, strong.

"Well," I remarkt, "unlest I wuz marrid to her, I ruther sumbody shood be thar. The ginrul apinyun uv the naberhood"—

"Dam the naberhood!" he replied, "thar's no naberhood in the kais."

With that the argymint drapt, and we all squandud off to our sevril apartmints.

I has give you this a kount, Billy, not becaus I deams the idee uv settin on the bank uv a kreek all day with a gearl ar enything very aridginul or calculatid to instruck you mutch, but becaus it shose you how remarkabul is the mines uv the peepul of Washintun. Cert'ny evrything and evrybody heer is strandge, and, as

Mr. Argruff sais, *swi genris*, which is the latten for pekewlyer. Uv the akewaintuntsis I has lately maid, nun is mo intrestin and talkativ than Mr. Hicmun, which he's vulg'ly called Bo', tho' I've nuver seen him with a lady yit. He chargis a quarter uv a dollur to be intojuiced to you, and runs his tung like a wheet fan, like he wuz feerd you woodint let him git throo. His face is fross bit and rinkled powful, and he's got him a sharp, onnachrul eye. I nuver sees him, which I do see him mos't evry day, hobblin long the street with his shorl, and his stripid britchis, and his bung'd-up feet, but my reckoleckshun terns to things neer Kerdsvil, which is this:.

Ole Cap'n Sinker had him a hoss, naim Wrankin, wunst a fine saddil hoss, but bein mitey ole, terned him outen a ole feel to die, in the naberhood uv a ole tumbil doun terbarker hous. He had plenty to eet, but what he eet dun him no good, and he got leener and leener every day, till you cood uv hangd a hat on his hip boans, is they say. Whenuver old Wrankin lade doun, which was ofting, the buzzuds got arfter him, atacting him, dartin at him, and peckin at his eyes. Finely po ole Wrankin sufferd so mutch from these onslots he got nurvus, and ef a clowd cum over the sun he thot it wuz the shadder uv a buzzud in the ar, and went into the terbarker hous and shet the do' to keep fum bein eet befo his tiem. Well, wun day it cum close clowdy all day, and po ole Wrankin thinkin the hevins wuz alive with buzzuds, staid in his terbacker hous, and shet the do', and thar dide, and bout nite cum a clap uv thunder, nockt doun the ole hous, berrid him, and maid a fine monyumint fer him. Well, Mr. Hicmun remines me of that ar ole skragly ole hoss and that are ole tumblin-doun ole hous, which methinx he can't hole up long. He ar sertny ar a man uv jeenyus, whitch I feals a fealin uv simp'thy fer him.

I sees, Billy, I'm libel to run offn the trac is a injine on the Sowthside rail-rode, as I hasint tole you uv nuthin hardly I begun to tell you uv. But wun thing mo I must narate year I quits this heer epistul, which ar is follers:

I tellin Mayan I had a grate sekret, which I fines I can't keep nuthin frum her uv my oan, she idviesd me not to truss nobody, not eavin Mr. Argruff, and p'tickly Oans and Melloo, which she sais they nose too much enyhow; but to tend to my oan afars myself. So I thot I'd nock aroun and taik pusnul observashin uv evrything, speshly uv Kongris. So I gose and gose way up the streat in the mist of a grate dust that blose heer konstunt like thrashin uv wheet, and gose up to the Captul. I jes tell you the Captul heer ar a nuther site to the Captul in Richmun, but the yard, which its fashnuble to call it grounds in a sitty, ar about pritty mutch the saim, sicxs uv wun and haf duzen uv the uther. The bildin ar about is long is frum Baldin's ole sto (they tells me he's dun move doun to the plank rode) to the Piskypil cherch in Kerdsvil. Speekin to Oans a bout this bildin' he sais its like awl gall, devided into three parts. But I tole him that a gall were wun thing, whitch it wuz a blarther.

"Ah," he sais, "but, you see, I sed awl gall; awl gall ar a difrint thing frum gall; awl gall ar a Frentchmun's gall, whitch it's totely difrint from a Emerrykin's gall, bein heap mo uv it; and that's the resin Frentch peepul is the most gall-ant in the wirl." And that ar a spesmin uv wun uv Oansis punz (pun, meenin a wird which meens sumthin eltse) on the wird g'lant, whitch is spry, 'tentive to the gearls.

Howuver, the Captul bildin heer ar imments. Taint finisht tho', and the top uv the middel uv it ar adorned with a surkil uv pillers whitch being part white and part black, looks like trees whitch has bin beltid, sum beltid and sum burnt. You has to go up a site uv steps to git into the bildin, and the ferst thing you cums to ar a marvel monyumint, representin nakid humin becins standin roun a post whitch has a numbo uv split pitchers stuck to the sides uv it—and this monyumint are bilt rite in the middel uv a pon uv stagnunt warter, rite grean; and what's mo' the pon warnt thar oridginully, but wuz maid thar to bild the monyumint in. You wont bleeve me, Billy, but its the fac, and shows what fool peepul thar is in this worl. Thar's a iun railin roun the pon, and when I lookt over it into the pon, I seen the cook had been thorin slops into it, p'tickly carrots. But twarnt carrots, Billy; what you reckin twuz? Why, gole fish, whitch the pon is full uv um, and thay lade so still in the warter I thot twuz carrots. Gole fish is a kine uv yaller belly pearch, only thar backs is yaller, or ruther red too.

While I wuz a lookin at the pearch, fine ladies and membus uv Kongris kep on passin me goin up stars into the parler, which is alwais in the secund story, the parler is in toun. Feelin moddis, I detumined to go in the kitchin and chat with the kook, whitch I hoped she wuz a fat ole nigger womun, like a kook orter be, tel I wuz envitid up stars with the cump'ny. I past on by a marvil tombstone running warter under the bridge, got into the hous and lookt and lookt for the kitchin, whieh dernd ef I cood fine it. I ass'd a man goin by totin uv books, but he pade no atenshun to me. I tride a heap uv do's; all lockt. Finely, I thot I'd go up stars enyhow, and went up, and when I got thar it lookt mo like

doun stars than doun stars did.   Peerd like twuz a seller, with big
dubbel posses* uv rok, and a skewpt out seelin, and heap uv
bocksis, and trash, and wun thing and a nuther layin about.  Peepul wuz passin, a few uv um, but not likin to ixpose my igro-
nounce, I sais nuthin to um.   It were rite dark in thar, and I went
aroun and aroun twell pren'ly I cums to whar it were lighter, and
ternin throo a glass do', found a par of twistid steps goin up hier
yit in the bildin.  ' I wuz a goin on up, but hapnin to look over my
shoulder I seen a nuther glass, and throo it peepul, which I node
it were Kongris.   Aproachin the do,' a m'latter man settin inside
halls it rite open with a roap, and I goes in uv koas, feelin pritty
imbarist, and not seein uv much fer a tiem.   When I cum too a
little, I seen a small room, with a holler sealin runnin up in a
keervd maner, mogny fernicher, a few peepul, and roun the room
at reglar pints, a number uv busters uv grate men.   Buster is the
likeniss, hed, fase, neck, and peece uv the brest uv a man, chopt
out uv white marvil, with a bottum part sumthin like the bottum
uv a wine glass, to set it on.   Behine a long, levil, mogny bannister, set sum uv the kuyustist humins in exzistunts.   Of all and uv
all, they wuz the beet.   Ugly?   Blessed fathers!  I shood jedge
they wuz; and ole, and rinkildy, and drest in black silk apuns,
with tremendus sleeves, settin thar behine that ar bannister, still is
deth.   Yu've see sevin nor ate mud turkils squottid on a log, and
yu've see sevin nor ate ole tukky buzzuds settin on a lim' of a
tree; well, that is pecisely like them ole fellers settin behine that
ar bannister.

A gristly kine uv a man wuz a standin on the flo'in frunt of sum
tabils, trine to pint out a fac or ixplain sumthin ruther to them ole
*Posts.

turkils and buzzuds, which they didn't taik no intrus in what he
sed, 'pearin to be sleep mostly, but sum uv um readin. I shood
uv hav jedged the man on the flo to be a loryer ef he hadin bin
so eesy and natchrul like—he did'n rar nor he did'n rip, nor beller,
nor rampooge, nor tar his shert—he warnt a bit like our loryers
which I has seen plenty av um, at Buckingame kote. I tride and
tride to compren whut this fello on the flo' wuz a saying; but all
I cood doo I coodin taik no mo ingziety in it then the mud turkils
afosed.

"And this ar Kongris," I sais to myself. "Well, dern Kongris,"
and I lef.

Goin out by the glass do' which the m'latter man he pulled opin
agin with his string, I cums, at the foot uv the windin stars, to a
ole man sellin appils, cakes, pize, and so foth. I bot a par uv pize,
and ass'd fer sumthin to drink. The ole man sed he did'n had
nuthin but sum logger beer.

"Enything like p'simmum beer?" I sais.

He did'n seem to understan me, so I sais:

"Gimme sum enyhow." And he gimme sum, and I tastid it,
and it jes squirted itself spontainyusly outin me all over him, saim
is ef I'd bin a surrindge.

"No wunder you calls it logger beer," I sais, fuyus; "ef it taint
stump warter I wisht I may be dad shimd," whitch it ar, Billy.
And I lef.

What mo I seen uv Kongris I resurves. I've rit anuff fer wun
tiem, certin.

Luv to Unc' Jim. 'Member me to Kayine and An' Locky.

Rispeckfully and afeckshuntly yose,<br>
MOZIS ADDUMS,

## FIFTH LETTER.

MOZIS ON KANSAS.  INSIDE VIEW OF POLITICAL LIFE.  MIZ
HANSCUM AND MAYAN.

DEAR BILLY:

Billy that warnt no Kongris I seen, twarnt nuthin
but the Spreame Kote, which I shood uv knode it in a minnit ef
that ar loryer had hiseted the saddil skeerts uv his mental anemil
and socked the rowels uv his vois into the intestins uv his argymint, as is the fashin uv the mo notid as well as uv the yung and
asspirin members uv the roorul bar.  Uv the reeul Kongris thar
is a par uv um, bein 2, wun small wun called Sennit, and wun big
wun calld Hous.  But lets furst igzamin the struckcher uv the
Spreame Kote of the Yewnited Staits uv Emerryky, which it
shall be a breef expositchun, quite breef.

You buy a par uv plow lines from—well, say Ned Sinker in
Fomvil.  They turns out to be rottin in the twiss, and you refusis
to pay fer um.  You git sude, and jedgemint goes agin you.  You
apeals, and the sute goes on from Kote to Kote, hier and hier,
untwell it gits way heer into the Spreame Kote, sichuwatid under
the Washintun Kongris bildin, as afosed.  Thar it stops, it's got
to the las' notch on the beam uv the mighty stilyuds uv Jestis.
Nine human turkils in silk gounds takes the kais in hand, and
when they've sed thar say, nuthin mo kin be sed; you got to shet

up, pay fer yo ole wuthless, ole plow lines, and a heap mo besides.
At lees this ar Mr. Argruff's explaynashun, which he giv it to me
sune arftur the advencher related in the finis, the eend uv a former
episil.

As to Kongris, to return. Thar's a par uv um, Hous and Sennit. Ef wun are calld Hous, the uther orter be called Hut or
ruther Volt, sais Oans, becos Sinnit ar a mean littil gougdout
darkey hole, wharas Hous ar a risplendid and imments apartmint, got up withont regard to coss, and full of the finis paint and
gildin, jined together in the mos' startlin and ixquizit tace, saim is
a ritch, a brite and a brilyunt quilt, which a stewjus ole maid in
the kuntry, havin a igzistunts litrully bloated with spar time, she
maiks it, and sens it, with meny aintchunt and vurginul teers, and
fond hoaps uv glowry, to the Anyul Farr at Richmun, whar it
taiks the pries or dont taik it, akordin to the mo or less pewrifide
sense uv the bewtyfull uv the Kumitty on quiltz fer the time bein.
Thus seth Oans, and I fobar to add nuthin to the critysism.

Sence heer I've bin, I've bin to Kongris a menyer time, and ef
I has lernt enything, which I has my douts uv it, it ar this. Ef
uver I do cum to Kongris, which I shill nuver do it is long is I
kin mall rails ot eet persimmuns, the fust thing I intends to do ar
pintidly to interjuice a nact to amend a nact that nuver wuz in-
titled a nact to permote the efeeshincy uv Kongris ; fur uv all peepul on the fase uv the erth to talk, and talk, and talk, and do
nuthin, they is the beet.

And Kanzis, Billy—goodness nose I wisht it wuz berrid under
Willis's mountin.  I do think it's enuf to maik a man cuss out
and quit the humin famly which has heerd what I has heerd on
this drottid subjick ; constunt, Billy, without no sessashin furuver

and furuver mo. Nar a tiem has I gone to Kongris, but strait-
way a man upriz and pode foth the viles uv his rath on Kanzis,
howlin at it like a houn when you blow the hon fer dinner,
yelping at it like a fice when he sees a straindge nigger cummin in the yard.

But I stans by my party in this heer matter, Billy. The
gloyus dimockrasy and Mister Wilyum Cannun (I hates rhe
vulgy way uv callin uv him Mr. Buck Cannun) is rite, pufficly
rite in thar psishun.

But I feels mitey bad about this Kanzis eny way, and the kuntry too. Things is cum to sich a pass that we ar ableged to cary
on the guvnurmint and exekeut the lors, under falts pretensis as
twuz; we cant do what we kno to be rite ixcep in the naim uv
them we kno to be doin rong, and the grate hoss cart of public
afars is a gointer stall pritty soon. It's bin a travlin up a mitey
ruff rode lattly enyway, the tail-bode is busted, and the most vallybil kontents is a joltin out wun arfter anuther powful fast. Befo
long, I'm afeard Mr. Wilyum Cannun will find his hosses is goin
too fast, and lookin roun to see what's the reesin, will fine the wag-
gin-body intily empty, the lode all gone cleen.

In Hous and Sennit, from time to time, I've see the mos distinguisht men uv the nashun, and bin astonisnt at thar close resemblunts to the rest ot mankine. But menyer grate man livs in
a common hous, like Unc' Jim for igsampil; so 'tis with the soules
of jeenyus, which most in ginrully speakin dwells in tenymints,
badly bilt at ferst, and soly in need uv new wetherbodin, white-
wosh, an mo brix on top uv the chimblys to bring um up to the
standud uv granjer.

I has scd thar is a close resemblunts bztween Kongrismen and human nacher is you find it layin about anywhar. To be kandid, Billy, they is wun and the saim thing, identykil, ripresentatives and men is. Git jam up aginst um, you can't tell um apart, to save yo life you can't.

I wuz struck with this remokabul fac freakwently when I has went into Honerbul Mr. Swomplans's room, and a pompus and mo' kunseetid ole fool than ole Swomplans nuver had pockits in a kote tail. Pusnully he's igzackly like Littleberry Huddilstun, igsept his head ar ball, but his carictur ar a mixture uv Ganwy's Yawk and Bell. Now tuther night:

Thar wuz thar in ole Swomplans' room three or fo yung Kongrismun, and bewtiful spesmins they wuz. Nuver in all my born dais did I heer sech cussin an swarrin and tellin uv joaks. They got to runnin wun nuther about their reekods. You see, Billy, soon's a man gose into pollitix everything he sais and duz is kep akount uv, and that akount is called reekod. So ef a pollytishun duz enything rong, his enymis goes to his rekod and pints out the fac, and the very plais and time whar he dun it, and he's got to tell mo lies than anuf to git shet uv it. So when they wuz all a talkin bout this, yung Mr. Joans he ups and swo' he had the damdis mos' butyfull reekod on erth. Then yung Bosin ript out and sed he wisht he may be teetotally swept into —— ef *his* reekod warnt p'yo* and spotliss is the senter page uv the sacrid album uv a virgin's soul. "D— it!" sais Joans, "how'd you vote on the Kanzis-Nebrasky bill? And cuss you, didin you maik a speech lass Summer in favur uv distributin the proceeds uv the public lans?" "You ar no better than an infunil No-Nuthin enyhow," ansers Bosin. So they went rippin and cussin at each uther

*Pure.

6

tell Swomplans he spoke up and tole um they wuz compormisin the dignity uv Kongreshnul carrickter. "What," sais he, "wood yo constitchyunts think ef they cood heer this undignifide, pofane, and vilent oltercashun?"

They both damd thar constitchyunts to the devil, and took a drink. They wuz cummensin at it agin, when little ole Melloo stopt um saying uv: "Gentmen, you ar both equilly grate, and yo reekods equilly immackulit, but listin to this." He red frum a paper he'd bin ritin, which went on to say that a telegraf dispatch just reseeved frum the grate Dimokratic Convenshun, then settin (imadjinin the year ateen-sixsty-ate) at Hayvaner in the Ilund uv Cuby, had anounst that ether the Rite Honnerbil Sennytur Bob Joens, or Guvner Tom Bosin had reseeved the unanmus nomina-shun fer Presydint.

"Uv koas you'll be electid," sais Melloo, "whichever gits it, and as things is goin on wun uv you will be boun to git it, and now I wanter know what you gointer do for me, yo ole and valyud fren and intmit kumpanyun?"

Bosin spok furst. He sais:

"I shall pursurve the dignity uv my stashin. I shall say, Mr. Melloo, I'm not unmineful uv the past. I recall the plesint hows uv yuth, when we wus frens togethur, as I'm yose now. But I o it to my kuntry and myself to make my adminystrashun gloyus, and to that eend I inten to slekt for my constitewshunul advisers, and for the princepel ripresentatives uv the ripublick abroad, the very ferst men in the nashun. My long akwaintunts with you will not justify me in assining eny uv theese psichins to Mr. Mel-loo. Nuvertheless you shell hav a post uv honur and uv profit.

Wharupon I'll hand you yo commisshin as consul to Livpool or Peekin."

Then Joans sed : "You aint goin to hear no such stuff is that frum me. Soon's you call on me at the White Hous, I am a gointer say, ' Peter,' (that Melloo's givin naim,) ' Peter, ole feller, how ar you. I'm d—d glad to see you. Taik a seet and set doun.' Then I'll send for a bottle uv Green Seal, and we'll both git is drunk is d—. And befo you go way, I'm gointer say to you like Ole Buck sed to Forny, ' taik whutuver you durn pleas.' And ef yu ar smart like Forny, and go in fur the publick printin, you shell hav it. I'm not goin to refuse you nuthin. It'll then be wuth about two milyuns a yeer, and ef we dont hav the tallest kind uv a time you may take my hat. We'll live like the Sardeens uv Annopolis,* becos I dont inten to git marrid, but I'm a gointer to have all the pritty wimmin in the Yunitid Statis bodin at the White House free uv charge ; and we'll rip rite throo fo' splendid yeers, certin and sho ! Joans may talk about his administrashin, but mine is gointer leave behine it a streak of glowry long is tail uv a comic and brite is a flash uv litenin. That's so. You may bet you life on it. The way for a man to maik his administrashin glowyus is to stan up to his frens like ole Jacksin and taik the responsibillity. Twont do for a Presydint to be squeemish and conshentshus. Conshents be d—d ! Ole Buck's tride that gaim, and it doant pay."

Billy, them's his very wurds. It's true he ware yung, both Joans and Bosin, but they ar upun a par with the ballunce, jest is smart and smarter than wun haf uv um. And that's the way grate men, Dimmocrats and all, go on when they ar by themselves

*Can Mr. Addums mean Sardanapalus ?

talkin bout thar kuntry, thar Presydent, and the responsibil duties
uv thar station like it warnt nuthin.   Dont you say a wurd about
this, you heer.   Ef uver it wuz to git out, the kuntry wood be
ruined and cleen ruinatid.   Nuver no members uv Kongris wood
cum heer no mo'.   Who cood truss um arfter talkin in that ar
way?   Why peepul in the kuntry, when they went to maik thar
speechis at a presink, woodint dar to come anigh um.   Wood
they, Billy?

Heer I've dun run away with mysef agin, like a ole hoss arfter
sum mischifus boy hav put a cuckly burrer under his tail.   But
pollytix ar a subjict the mos' prefoun, requirin abundunts uv time
and spais fer the proper treatmint and elucydashun uv it.   Ef
brevity are the sole uv wit, lenth are the upper-lether uv lojick,
which my mine ar very cleer on this pint tharof.        ·

I promist to tell you how I becum akwaintid with the ladis at
the Mintzpi Hous, which the way uv it were in these wise:   Wun
day, goin in to dinner, my sensis compleatly absorbd in absents
uv mine over the still mo futher puffeckskin uv my projick, rite at
the dinin room do' I run agin Miss Saludy Tringil, cummin a
dantsin out as ushil, like a duck swimmin up to mill-wheel, and
stumblin is I fell, I reecht out my han nachrilly to ketch sumthin,
and getherd up sum tabil cloth and sum frock and sum cheer,
which I think it muster bin the bac uv the cheer, becos I upset
Miz Hanscum backruds, brakin uv her plate and spillin uv a salt-
seller in my eye.   Thar it wuz befo the whole cumpny, and how
I got out'n it I swar ef I kno.   I nuver shell git over it when I
thinx uv it.   I kno I dident eat nuthin' that day, and were shamed
to go to tabil tel evrybody had lef', tel laitly.

Oans—I do like that Oans—he cum to me and cunsoled me,

and when my mine grajually settled, tole me twuz my dewty to
goe and apollygize like a gentmun.   The perpriety wharof I per-
seevd at a glants.   I assd him to give me a day to pepar my mine
for the undertakin, and when the day were past and gone, with
grate delibyrashun and fumness I adrest myself to the task, and
dun it.   Jest befo I left hoam on this expedishun you reckollect I
got me the finis kine uv a sute uv clothes maid in Fomvil, which
I reckin they ar eekul to eny maid enywhar, I dont keer whar.
Rambut for coats, and Forrer for britchis, the worl cant beet um.
And I had a par uv boots maid by Tony; kin mo be sed?

Araid in these garmints, I felt like a gentilmun, which I ar in
sperit ef not in apeerunts, and, with the help uv Oans, made my
apollogy soe satisfacktry, I soon becum a grate favrit with all the
ladis, aspeshly Miz Hanscum—powful atracktiv womun she is,
Billy.   Arfter a modrit amount uv izperymints, I felt as nachrul in
the Mintzpi parler is a steer in a patch uv clover.   I visitid thar
freakwintly, and sumhow or ruther I were alwais thode with Miz
Hanscum, which were the okashun wun nite uv this hapnin:

Didje ever hav a par uv dough-skin broad-cloth britchis, Billy?
How slik they is.   Well, I had on mine that nite, and whenuver
I has um on I cant help slidin my hans doun um, it feels so good
to the pam.   Settin talkin to Miz Hanscum, she ubzervd my
stroakin my britchis doun to the knees, like they wuz the necks uv
two blak hosses jes curry-combd and rubd down—ubservin this,
it atracktid her atenshun, and she sais:

" Those apeer to be very nise pantloons, Mr. Addums."

" Yes'm," I sais, " Forrer maid um."

Then she assd me who Forrer wuz, and I tole her, and that in-
dewsd her to queschn me sum mo, and mo yit, tel finely I giv her

my hole histry. I reckin twuz levin o'clock befo I got thoo, and every body ware gone out'n the parler ixcept us, and we wuz settin plegg-takid clost together, she lookin so warm and good out uv her brite eyes like she reely keered fer my welfar, and I feelin fine and puffickly kuntentid to stay rite thar, and ef enything a leetil closter, tel day. Jest then the do' opened and in cum Oans, evydently not ixpecting to find nobody. I spect he wanted to look at hisself in the long lookin glass they got thar running fum the flo' clean up to the seelin. Enyhow, the momint he seen us settin so intmit, he says quick "ixcuse me," and went rite out.

This kinder flustud me and I jumpt up, but Miz Hanscum she dident mine it a bit, but sais in a verry cam vois "set doun," and I set doun, and we went on talkin mo' intmit than uver. All uv a suddin, I jumpt up agin and sais, "excuse me," and run out, and dident hardly stop runnin tel I got into my oan room.

"What maid me do so singly?" you sais.

*Billy, she wuz arfter findin out my seekrit, shose you born she wuz!*

You dont kno theese peepul in Washintun, and how keen they is arfter a vallybil thing. Hadint I heerd how the cunnin roskuls fum the North inveegils members uv Kongris with pritty ladis? You cant fool me.

To tell the truth, Billy, this acurrants hapened only las' nite, and I got a grate mine to stop bodin at the Mintzpi. It's danjus.

But this mornin I got up and tole Mayan the intire suckumunce, desirin to hav a intellijint veu uv a womun's doins fum anuther womun. Mayan were dustin the mantil pees when I cummenst a tellin her, and she ternd roun and listined good tel I got cleen thoo. Then she ternd roun and commenst dustin agin. I waited, but she dident say nuthin. Gittin impayshunt, I sais:

"Warnt I rite in my conjeckshur?"

She kep on dustin, and sais in the mos' keerless manner:

"It's no seekrit the pritty lady's afther a tall, a tall."

"She aint so mitey dog-gon'd pritty," I sais, "but what were she arfter then?"

And reckin, Billy, she dident say she were arfter *me*. That bewtifull, ritch Miz Hanscum arfter me? The idee! Then I reekolectid Mr. Argruff sayin how all the ladies in Washintun wuz bleest to luv Mozis Addums, the bar cunsepshun uv which giv me a pane in the eye ball uv astonishtment. Verily, the world are straindge. Then I remembud the disparity uv our suckumunsis in life, *at presint*, and sais out loud,

"Sher!"

But Mayan she went on rubbin uv the mantil pees—she dun rub it all over two three times aready—not notesin me in the leese. Jest then my eye lit upon her han', and consoun me, Billy, ef it warnt the prittiest, littlist, whitist, well-formed han' in the world.

S'I, "Mayan, look heer. Thar's sumthin rong about you. That aint no servunt gearl's han'. That aint no han' customd to work."

Soon's I sed it, she snacht her han' away like a bee had stung it, and hid it. Facin roun, she lookt at me, white is a sheet, movin her lips, but sayin nuthin. Culler begins cummin to her cheek, yusully very rosy, and she broke out:

"Mozis Addums, you is the biggis goos in the wirld," an she fled, and wuz doun stars in a minnit.

The sentents abuv, she sed it in the very bess uv Inglish, like

me and you speeks it, and it starkled me.   I jumpt up and run
arfter her, callin her:

"Mayan, Mayan," I sais.

"Surr!" she replide, from way doun the steps.   It cum up
coas is the teeth uv a whip-saw, and it hert me that bad I went
and set doun on the bed for a nour befo I gits over it.

Billy, thar's sumthin rong about that gearl you may be boun,
and I'm not a gointer res tel I finds it out.

I shood uv have rit you this letter long ago but fer the arivil
heer uv Oans' par, a scrowgin ole gentilmun, long amost is the
toe-line uv a canel, havin uv ruther a pleasin fais all kivered with
har, and runnin all over toun like he was distracktid, and me and
Oans kontinyul runnin arfter him in a state uv painful mentil ingziety and ankwish, fer feer he'd loss himself or git hert.   Peepul
ort reely to be mo keerful how they 'low thees ole creturs to buss
loos from the ristraints uv the famly and fiside, and ixpose himself
to the temtashins uv fashnubil life in a sitty.   It's hily injuyus.

So far yu well, Billy, tel nex time,

MOZIS ADDUMS.

## SIXTH LETTER.

COCKRUN'S GALRY.   THE THEATER.   THE SMITHSONIUM.   BILL-
YUDS.   MR. ADDUMS'S FUST VISIT TO THE PRESYDINT.

DEAR BILLY:

Billy, my son, lemme give you a pees uv advise.
Ef uver you git tanguld with a wummun, nuver do you taik no
tiem to ontie no nots, nor ontangul nuthin; jes tar rite loos, and
ef you cant tar loos, pull out yo nife and cut the Gorjun Not and
travil.   Put yo fingurs in yo yeers and heer nuthen she's got to
say.   Ef you don't, bi jing! you gone, certin.

I kep on a bodin like a fool at the Mintzpi, the konsequince uv
which ware dezastrus in the ixtream.   Me and Miz Hanscum—
but nuver you mine a bout I and her.   But tware very plesint
thare at the Mintzpi.   In during uv them days, cum two marrid
ladis thar, the bewtifullist in the worl.   Ethur was anuf to nock a
man down with thare luvly body and mine, and both together was
more'n anuf.   In adishun uv them, cum a littil Trungil, sister uv
Miss Saludy, and she were one uv them ingajin veriety uv gearl
that draws you like a mustud plarstur, or a wagun and teem.
Cum, furthermo, a littil gal from Injanner, like a hed uv white
clovur, she were so far to look apun and so sweet!

I tell you, Billy, we all had fine tiems.   Havin plunjd into fashnubil life, I went on doun in the vawtix and kep on doun, furgit-

ing uv my skeam, furgiting uv everything. Sech is the way in Washintun, whar peepul, stid uv tendin to thar biznes goes to spendin uv munny and injoin uv themself like the wild. What with eatin and a drinkin and a smokin uv segars, and a goin to Kongris, and to the Patint Offis, the Theater, the Smithsonium, and Cockrun's galry, it ware gloyus. Time floo, and ixpensis wuz hevy.

This heer Cockrun's galry gits its naim from a white marvel gal, rite start bodily nakid, standin on a velvit stump in the fur eend uv a room filled with paintid pickchers. It's mighty pritty Billy, mighty pritty ; and I reckin about the best formdid gal in Emeriky.. I wisht I cood a seen her drest fur a Hop, and seen her set doun and talk. I jedge she'd a made a impreshin.

A Hop, Billy, air a danse they has every nite in the parlers uv the big tavuns. Oans, a roscul! carrid me the fust tiem to wun at the Mintzpi Hous, and bleevin what he tole me, und he doin uv the saim, thar we went a hoppin round the room like a cupple uv mainyaks, stid uv dansin as we ought to. Nuver did I heer peepul laf so senst I wer born.

The Smithsonium, whar the Cluk uv the Wether livs, with his insterments to mezure the ar and the rain, an tellin uv a hot day from a cole wun, you goes to to heer lecktchurs on vayus subjicks. Lecktchur air a kind uv sermun, without eny trimmins, no tex, no singin uv hims or prars or docksollygis. I heer a man thar lectchur whitch he had bin to the Noth Pole and staid thar two years. Oans sais he sed the Noth Pole ware a simmun tree full uv peckerwood nesses, but I dident heer him say so. Then agin, peepul goes to the Smithsonium fer no resin at all, except twuz to nock roun and look at a room full uv potrits uv Injuns. And I

K'

ubservd it for a cuyus fac that the peepul what goes to this bildin
in the day time, when thar aint no lecktchurs, is ginerully a yung
man and lady, whitch luvs mitely to be by themself, and the yung
lady is alwais very moddis, warrin uv a vale and turnin uv her hed
so you nuver kin see her fais. And I ubservd the saim uv yung
men and ladis, goin in pars and wandrin round in the seller uv the
Captul.

At the Theatur thar is fo' kind up plays. Thar's Trajidy, and
Komedy, and Fars, and Ballay. You've see a littil nigger, when
he thot no body warnt a notesin nv him, snatch a sweet tater out'n
the ashes and run roun the chimbly and goes to gobblin uv it up
quick befo' sumbody cums and ketch him. You've seen how he
blewd and suckd and puft and swet and skrude his feechurs and
popt his eye, cause the tater is so hot. Well, that's Trajidy—that's .
the way the main man, which ginerilly gits killd, duz, and peepul
sais it's very fine.

You've see a self-cunseetid, nonsensicul po' gal jes frum skool,
cummin fer the fust time to a littil gethrin, a candy pullin or the
like uv that. Two or three bows gits to runnin on to her, and
you've see how she riggils and twisses and lafs, and lafs and lafs at
nuthin at all. That's Komedy, and the main wumun duz igzackly
that way, which ameuzis the peepul very mutch.

As fer Fars, that's a kind uv short Komedy, a boundin fer the
mose part, ef my reckolechshin surves me, in nasness uv idee and
speech. Sum uv um is pritty funny tho.

But the Ballay takes um all down. Dingd if it dont beet my
time. Ballay is dansin on the stage, and sich dansin! I'll be
blamed ef uver I see or dreemd uv. I went to the fust wun with
Oans, which sed we must git seets neer the stage, rite by the pen

whar the fiddlurs and men blowin on the Frentch horn and beetin
uv drums—all uv which is called Orkistur—sets. The lady that
was goin to do the best dansin were naimed Seen-yo-reen-er Rol-
lar. She wer a bewtiful black har'd Spanish lady, and soon
arfter we set doun, and the music had playd and the curtin rolld
up, she cum out like nuthin you uver imajind. Mayniffysent,
Billy, with a par uv wings to her nakid shoaldurs. Her frock
were spangild with dimunds, it were white is a clowd and fine is a
fog, and I wish I may be dernd ef it cum to her knees. I skeersly
know what I shell call them things in a lady which I shell call
legs in a man, but whatuver they is, in her cais they wuz splendid, eakul amost to them thar uv Cockrun's marvel gal, and
makin the cole chills run over you to look at um.

Well, ser, she went a skippin and a hoppin and a pirootin aroun
on the flatfom uv the stage, like a hummin berd, and pritty soon
she cum rite in frunt uv me cleen to the edge uv the stage, facin
uv the congregashun, and shot her foot rite smack up to the seelin.
The owdashus, onmanerd thing! in cumpny too! Ef you had a
stobd a derk thoo and thoo my hart, it coodent uv jumpt no mo'
than when she dun it. I leetil mo' to faintid. Oans he lafft rite
out, and the congegashun hoorawd and clapt, and stompt like
fewry. She kep on a doin uv it, and a feller drest tite is his skin
cum out and flung her over his hed and dun I dunno what all,
and the peepul hoorawin and a goin on wuss than befo'.

I were so shamed I darsent hardly look up, but the ladis and
gentilmen belongin to the first famlis uv Washintun hily apruved
uv it all. You kin jedge uv yo oan kunclushins in the case what
must be the nacher of Washintun sosiety. ‖

In adishin to these heer amewsmints, the men peepul uv Wash-

intun have a way uv a spendin uv thar spar tiem in the day that is
very kuyus.  It is a playin uv a gaim by the naim uv the gaim
uv billyuds.  They takes a tremendus pianner and takes out all
the insides—the music fixins—and kivers the hole top uv it with
a green cloth, makin a big tabil uv it, with the edges of the tabil
turnd up like the edges of a stew pan.  At every wun uv the
cornders and in the middle uv the two long sides uv the tabil is
put a rettykewl, makin uv six rettykewls in all.  On the tabil thar
is fo balls, two white and two red.  One uv the white balls is got a
fly spec on it, which fer the resin they call it a black ball.  The
fellers that's a goin to play, taiks in thar hand a whiteoake whip
staff without eny thong at all, but havin the eend uv it pintid with
a littil pees uv soul lether a bout the sise uv a ten cent pees.
These heer whip staffs is called Qs.  Each feller taiks his Q,
chorks the soul lether on the eend uv it, and perseeds to job the
balls at wun nuther and into the rettykewls on the sides and cornders uv the tabil.  Over the tabil a passel uv white and black
nutmegs is strung on a wier to count the game.  A nigger stands
by with a pole havin a fiddle bridge stuck to wun eend uv it, to
snatch the balls out uv the rettykewls and put um back on the
tabil and keep the gaim with the nutmegs.  And wood you bleeve
it, Billy?  the peepul uv Washintun play at this fool game all day
and all nite!  You may talk a boute the igronunce uv kuntry foax,
but I'll swar they aint to be cumpard with toun peepul.

I shell now tell you uv my ferst visit to the Presydint, which
happind sum tiem ago, but I has bin ruther techy on the subjic,
and thot I woodent tell you nuver.  But I will.

You see in prosekewtin uv my mane desine in cumin heer, I
maid cute inkwiris rellatif to my skeam, and cunclewdid from
7

whut I heerd, it were best to go rite too the fountin hed, that is
the Presydint, Mr. Wilyum Cannon himself.  I had sum konversashin with Oans on this pint.

S'e.  "Is it a matter uv much impawtense?"

S'I.  "Uv the utmus."

S'e.  "Then yo bess way will be to see the Presydint privitly.
I kin mainidge it very eazy for you."

S'I.  "I shell be a thousun tiems a bleegd to you."

S'e.  "Not at all."

So that very nite we drest up cleen and startid.  Stid uv goin
up the Avnew, we went doun in the dreckshun uv the Captul.

S'I.  "You goin rong."

S'e.  "No.  We inten sein uv the Presydint privitly, you kno.
Uv koas we dont go to the White Hous whar evry body goes,
but we gits to see him privitly at the dwellin uv a fren uv his whar
he goes uv a nite on speshil biznis."

We went on doun by Broun's Tavun and the Gnashnul, and I
reckin twuz a squar further.  Thar we went in a opin passidge
and up a par uv steps, and the fust thing I know we cum to a iun
do'.

"Thunderashin!" I sais, "what's this!"

"This ar a iun do'," sais Oans, "to keep the No Nuthins and
Plug Uglis from a cumin in heer and a killin uv him."

"Jes, so," I sais.  "Consoun thar soles!  I'd like too see um
try it while I'm heer."

Thar were a roap with a tossil to the eend uv it hangin by the
do', which Oans ketcht it and ringd a bell inside.  Then a leetil
Veneshin blind in the middle uv the do' slatcht opin, a feller
looked thoo it, and seein it were Oans opined the iun do', and we

walkt in. Rite into the mos bewtifull poller, Billy, you uver see, full uv splendid fernicher, paintins uv the Possils and Marters, and a lady huggin uv a tolibly nakid baby, a heap mo things, and sum sevril gentilmen a reedin uv newspapurs.

S'I, trimblin, "Whar is he?"

S'e. "In the nex room."

I lookt and thar wuz anuther poller, prittier then the ferst, with a heap mo pictchers, splendid lookinglassis, and eny quantity uv gentilmen settin roun a tabil whar thar were anuther gentilmun doin uv sumthin I coodin see. Up over the hed uv the gentilmun behine the tabil wer a paintin uv a temendus Tiger, and I notist arfterwuds thar wer a Tiger paintid on the carpit uv both pollers.

Oans seein me lookin at the Tiger sais;

"This hous are the privit rezidints uv the Minister uv Bengall, and that's why he's got the pictcher uv the Tiger, becaws the Tiger ar the emblim uv the Bengall peepul jes like the Egil is the emblim uv the Emerrykin peepul."

"To be sho," sais I, "but," I sais, "aint thar a mighty heap uv seegar smoke here? and I heer a powful rattlin goin on at that ar tabil and I think I distinguisht the soun uv a oath."

"Oh!" he sais, "the Minister uv Bengall is a fine feller and lets evry body do is they please."

"Rite whar the Presydint is?"

"Sertin, the Presydint dont keer."

"But," I sais, "who's that littil ballheddid yaller man in the jump-jackit, standin thar? Pears like he's waitin on sumbody."

S'e. "That's a very distinguisht man. That's Dred Scot, the Envoy Extrawdinerry and Plennypotencherry from Sain Dominger, that the Spreame Kote made sich a fuss a bout."

S'I. "I think I has heerd the naim befc. He aint white tho, Oans."

S'e. "Sertny not. He's a Dommynicker man."

"But he wasnt speckild, Billy ; he were regler yaller, like eny mlatter."

Oans maid me taik a seegar, and took me to a side bode whar thar wuz evry sort uv licker set out, and giv me a drink uv prime whiskey, and then we took cheers by the fier and smoakt. I lis-tened good, and I dont think I uver heerd sich swarrin in the next room in my life, ixcept in ole Swomplanzis room that nite, when the yung Kongrismen Joans and Bosin wuz thar. I tole you uv it, Billy. Then thar wer a kontinyul rattlin and a rattlin.

The man a settin behine the tabil would say, "Awl reddy ?" "Awl set?" and then sech anuther goin on, good*ness!* One feller sais "Hold!" anuther sais "Hold yo hosses." "Dont tern," sais another. "Take them red wuns out'n the pot and put um behine the tray." "Let *them* run to the dews." And they kep a rattlin and a rattlin. A feller sais "Roll!" anuther sais "Rip um, dam um !"

Then they all shet up, and a minnit arfter cummenst a cussin worse than uver.

"By G—d! I raked him fo and aft." "Took him, dam him." "Well, I fell fer menny a shad." "That's a dam sweet Jack, aint it?" "Yes, a h—ll uv a Jack !" "I've bin a buckin against the— thing all nite, and d— me ef he aint took me evry tiem." "I tole you so; nobody but a —— fool woud a kep on when he seen um runnin wun way all the tiem." "Well, I dont want nun uv yo advise," and so on, and so on ; and sich a rattlin and a rattlin.

I sais to Oans,

"In the naim of sense whut's the meenin uv this heer rackit?"

"Oh!" he sais, "that's nuthin but diplomesy."

Which he ixplaind diplomesy to meen the quorlin uv grate men when they tries the destiny uv nashins with keerds.

"Well," S'I, " who's the man behine the tabil?"

"That's Mister Deeler."

"Yes, I heerd um call him Mr. Deeler, but who's Mr. Deeler?"

"The Minister from Bengall, uv koas."

"Well, he *hav* a forrin look," I sais.

Then he tole me the naims uv all uv um, but when I assd him to interjuice me to the Presydint, he tole me to wait tel the diplomesy ware over. I assd him then to pint him out to me, and he pintid at him, but I coodint see him owin to the crowd, which kep increesin, tho sum went out okashinally. The cussin and the swarrin and the smokin went on wuss and wuss at the tabil.

Presintly ole Mr. Dred Scot cum in with a yung persun that sertny ware a nigger, tho Oans swo he wuz a Injun Printz from Centril Emeryky, (eny how he had wooly har,) and Dred Scot he tole um supper ware reddy. Immejitly most uv um quit thar diplomesy and went in a fer room back. Sum remaned at the tabil with Mr. Deeler from Bengall. I wuz a wotchin uv um goin in to supper, when Oans he techt my arm and sais,

"Thar he is; dont let him see you a lookin at him."

And thar he set, Billy, the Cheef Majistrait uv the Yunitid Staits, which I thought his har were gray, but twuz blak, died, Oans sed, fer an evenin party, a powful dark cumplected man, imposin in apeerunce, a settin in a cheer a reedin uv a paper.

Fergittin uv what Oans tole me, I stard at him like enything, and he ketcht me. When he walled his great big black eyes at

me, Billy, I ware reddy to give rite up, thar wer sumthin so over-
powrin in the idee uv being lookt at by a Presydint, I coodn keep
my eyes offen him, and, seein what a fool I ware, he got up and
cum rite at me. . I were goin to run, but Oans hilt me.

Sais he, in the plesint vois uv affability and a smilin at the saim
tiem.  Sais he,

"Wont you walk in and take supper?   You'll find a very good
supper in the nex room.  Walk in."

S'I, "I'm a thousin tiems ableeged, but ef you'll please to ixcuse
me, sir, I aint hongry."

"Well," he sais, "walk in with yo' fren', and taik a cup uv cof-
fee, a glass uv wine, or you and your fren' kin taik sumthin here
at the side-bode."

Oans he farly pulled me away.   I dident wanter go a tall, the
Presydint he talkt so frenly, and then agin I deside to see him on
privit biznis, you kno, but Oans he sed it ware kuntrary to ettyket
to see him on privit biznis befo we eet.

Well, sir, we went into suppur, and by the livins! they had
thar mighty nigh evry thing that uver went doun the neck uv
man—beef, muttin, vensin, ham, terky, dux (uv a kine they calls
canvis bax,) fouls, oshters, homny, pesurves, pickil, vayus kines
uv bred, inclewding uv buckwheet cakes and waffuls, selry, plums,
ammuns, filbuts, and evrything in the werld to drink, from tea up
to the squirtin kine uv wine they call shampane.   The diplomesy
men, sum uv hoom lookt like I had seen um befo in Kongris wuz
a talkin uv pollytix, cussin and eetin like the dickuns, and me and
Ooans jes wadid rite in and eet and drink the squirtin wine tel we
like to bustid.   Nuver did I injoy sech a meel befo, the memry
uv it remanes with me evin yit.

Arfter suppur, feelin fine and fraid uv nuthin, I walkt up to Mr. Dred Scot, the yaller Dommynicker man, and tole him I wantid to see the ole man privitly. I calld the Presydint the "ole man," jes to show Scot how I warnt no strainger in the plase, and felt apun turms uv equolity with eny man.

Scot he sed the ole man ware gone to bed—retide for the nite, and Oans he cummin up about that tiem giv the Envoy Ixstraw-dinnerry from Sain Dominger a quorter, and what astonisht me, he took it, and sed we must "call agin." And we leff without me seein uv the Presydint in privit a tall. But I ware glad to hav see him eny way, becaws he perduced a favable impreshin upon me. He ware sertny very amebil and perlite.

Yose constuntly,

MOZIS ADDUMS.

## SEVENTH LETTER.

MOZIS AND MAYAN. A RESOLUTION. A FIGHT. MOZIS ARREST-
ED. HORRID TIMES. THINGS CLEAR OFF. SECOND VISIT TO
THE PRESYDINT.

DEAR BILLY :
I cum hoam fum a visitin uv the Presydint in high
sperits. The squirtin wine had got into my hed, which it felt like
a hous-raisin wuz a goin on somewhar, or ruther like the publick ·
mind ware roustid apun a impawtunt subjick of general intris.
Thar apeared to be a goad eel uv ixsitemunt, and I had a inlarged
vue, as it twuz fum sum mounting eminents. Oans he poked off
to one plais or anuther, levin me to entur my bodin hous aloan,
but puffickly cuntentid and rezined. The fust thing I heard it
were littil ole Melloo a skratchin on his fiddil and a makin uv pre-
haps the sicknest and horowblis souns in the worl. He can't play
no fiddil. The next thing I dun, I run aginst Mayan in the dark
—snatcht her rite up, carrid her in my room, shet the do', and
lockt it, detummined to diskuver the reesin she spoke Inglish
sumtiems and then agin Irish sumtiems, or dy in the atemp. She
ware solid, Billy, is a wannut stump, wayin, I jedged, a hundud
and fotty poun neet, but she warnt nuthin but a shuck boalstur to
me, feelin is I did. Mo rover, it ar a known fac that a man, mo
ptickly ef he ar yung, kin toat mo gal, mo ptickly ef *she* ar yung

and pritty, then uv eny uther substunts uv nater, whether uv the anemil, vedjetuble, or minrul kingdum; and I candlely bleeve that eavin a par uv muels kin haul fo', to one, by weight, uv gearls to eny uther kine uv truck.

I hadin seen Mayan to speak to her fer I dunno when. So I set her doun on a cheer, lit my lamp, set doun myself, and lookt at her and sed nuthin. I dident know what too say. I had dun dun the thing almost befo' I knowd it, thout knowin how I cum to do it, and had nearly forgot what I dun it fer, igzackly. She lookt at me mad is fier.

"Is it outin yo sensis ye ar?" she sais.

I shet my mouth hard.

"I do be thinkin its murther ye ar arfther."

I sais not a sillybul.

She jumpt at the do' like litenin, but I ketcht her, took the key out and put it in my pocket. She fit desprit, but I hilt her, and finely set her back in the cheer agin, while she set thar pail is flour, pantin fer breth, and lookin at me with her black eyes like she'd burn me cleen up. I set puffickly still and dident bat my eye wunst. Then she giv up. She took to cryin like I don't warnt to see nobody cry agin. I drord my cheer up and took her han; she thode me off like I'd been a mockersin snaik and cryd mo then uver. I tried it agin; she thode me off agin feerser then the fust time, and kep on a cryin. I getherd a.pipe, filled it with that good Linchbug tobarker, and pretindid to smoak. But I ware skeerd. I ware feard she'd kill herself, she cryd so. I begged her, I sais:

"Mayan, for the Lord's saik don't cry so. I don't mean you

no harm. I'd die ten thousin deths befo I'd hert a har uv yo hed."

But that maid her wuss. So thar we set,—she a cryin and I a trimblin. You may depen I repentid what I had dun. I got up and opined the do', onlockt it, and spred it wide opin. She stopt in a minnit. She got up to go out, still a sobbin, but makin no noise. I put my han on her shoalder very gently, and sais :

"Pleas don't go, Mayan.'"

She didin pull mighty hard, so I jes led her back eesy, and set her doun agin, and she commenst a cryin but not like befo—peard like it come mo softer to her. I hitched up my cheer clost to her, tryin to taik her han, but she pulld it away, slowly tho'. Arfter while, she lookt up at me, her buteful black eyes full uv teers, and sais mighty sorrerful and reproachful, she sais :

"Mistur Addums, you ortint to do me so."

"Thar now, thar now!" I sais, jumpin spang outin my cheer ; "thar now! I ketched you. By gravy!" I sais, "that's no Irish talk, and you aint no Irish nuther. Now you got to up and tell me evry single bit about yoself. Yu've bin a possumin long anuf, and you shant go a step tel you tell me. You sertny shell not."

She lookt at me like she'd look me throo. Then she smiled a littil bit uv a smile, but her eyes still full of teers, and sais sollum is possybil :

" Then shet the do'."

I shet it, quick.

"Lock it," she sais.

I lockt it. I ware comin back to taik my seat, when she sais in the saim sorrerful vois ;

Hadint you better blow out the lite? Some uv the gentilmen might wanter cum into see you."

"Well!" thinks I, "this beets the beet." But I blode out the lite and sais nuthin.

Then she made me to go with her to the back winder, whar the moon was a shinin over the houstops, and thar we set doun, and she tole me everything. I shill tell you awl about it sum these dais. Shes a rispectable girl, Billy, hily ejukatid, and uv good parrintidge—a reel lady, in fac. Her father is a kine uv preecher, which they calls in Iland a Q'rate; gittin monsus po' pay, sumthin like a sirkit rider, which he's a gentilman nuvertheless. She ware a high-sperritid gearl, which rund away becos her father marrid her step-muther and she coodint git along with her. When she cum to this kuntry, she took to talkin like the rest uv the charmber mades, and took to doin uv hous wurk, becos she sed it ware the ferst thing that come to hand, and, arfter tryin it, she liked it becos it kep her helthy and in good sperits. Her farther have sent her munny to come hoam repeetidly, but she wont come, on a count uv her step-muther. She staid in Knew Yawk a year, then come heer, whar she's bin goin on 2 years. This ar a meer outlyin uv the fax uv the case, Billy, but it's the plane truth, and nuthin elts. What a pictcher uv the sersiety uv the grate sitty uv Washintun. A white gearl, a pritty gearl, a reel lady, with fotty times the sense uv the womun that hires her, waitin on evry Tom, Dick and Harry! It's too bad, too bad intily! and ortent to be so no longer. I ixpec thar's menny anuther po gearl jes like Mayan is, and she sais so too.

We had a long, long happy talk thar by the winder. I declar, Billy, I nuver felt so sosherbil and sattisfide in my life. She seamed to plais so much confidents in me, like I wuz her bruther, or kussen, or sumthin. It tetched me to the co'. A cloc striked 2 befo' we partid, and then I didn want her to go, but she sed she must. I giv her my lamp, she lit it, tole me not to say nuthin to nobody bout what she had tole me, tole me good nite, and when she got part way up the steps stopt, and smilin doun at me tole me good nite agin. Oh Billy, Billy, hunny ar wirmwood cumpard to the speech uv wimmin sumtimes. Goodness nose! it doo appear to make a feller's hart melt in his bress.

I didn sleep nun that nite; I didn eavin ondress. I jes laid on the bed thinkin, thinkin, in a sort uv trants, and shood uv hav laid thar fur uver, ef, a bout the braker day, Mr. Argruff, he hadinter cum in. His face ware gassly and evil beyond amost enything. He dropt into a cheer and bowd his hed upon the tabil and giv a grone—sich a grone! it friz the blud in my very vanes. Then he looks up, like he dident know whar he ware, and begins to cuss hissful orful, orful, and call hisself fool, fool, fool, like he wisht he cood tar his hart out and distroy hisself with his own langwidge. I jumpt offin the bed and run to him and begd him to tell me what the matter wuz. He give a start saim is ef he'd bin shot. Billy, he ware drunk. His breth had that ar green, pizenus odur uv a man that drinks a heep and constunt. He thought he ware in his oan room, and when he foun whar he wuz, and seen me good, he knew me, he begins a cryin, and *sich* cryin—Mayan's warnt nuthin to it. It ar a turrabil thing fer to see a man cry is he dun. It mighty nigh killed me, cos I has a high apinyun uv Mr. Argruff.

When he got over his fit, at least the wust uv it, he let me know all bout it. Betwixt his intruption uv his remarks with fust a cryin

and then a cussin uv himself, I cood barly make out whut he sed,
ixcept it twus this: That he were in love with a yung lady, which
I shant call her name, and had coted her, and she had kickt him,
and he goes and gits drunk, and the fust thing he node he had
dun gone and got in bed with her farther, and tole him how he
loved his dawter and awl about it.   Did you uver heer uv sich a
thing, Billy?   It ware enuf to make him cuss hisself, and mo' too.
When he cum to tell about it, I thought he'd a gone distracktid
with shaim he ware so mad with hisself.

I cumfutted him the bess I cood, which it ware ruther po' cum-
fut, tried to maik him lay down in my bed, but he wooden let me,
so I tuk him to his oan room, ondrest him, put him to bed, and
left him.

My hart ware hevvy is led, thinkin how the bess peepul in
Washingtun seamd to be flicktid with sum dredful habbet or
anuther, and how retchid a life the happiest uv um leeds, when I
cum away frum the hous whar Mr. Argruff boded.   I felt like I
wantid to git away frum thar and git hoam whar thar wuz sum
quiat and pees, and whar peepul, ef they aint smart, is sertny
natchrul and contentid.

When I cum to the Mintzpi Hous, and had eet my breckfuss,
Miss Saludy Trungil and her little sister got arfter me, pleggin
me most to deth.   Fust they tole me my sweetart, Miz Hanscum,
(which she nuver wuz no sweetart uv mine a tall,) had dun rund
away with a feller, and gone posably to the devil.   And I dident
keer ef she had.   Then they kept a makin me tell bout my visit
to the Presydint, and the mo I tole how kinely the Presydint
treated me and how much I wer pleesed and all, the mo they lafft
and lafft, untel I thought nar one uv um had good sense.   No

wonder they lafft; for ef you bleeve me, Billy, I hadint seen no
Presydint a tall, and the hous which I thought it ware the privit
resedints uv the Ministur uv Bengall, wuz what they call a Forrer
Bank.  Forrer is sumtimes called Farrow and sumtimes Fareo,
and it ar a gaim uv cards, playd out uv a kind of Seedlitt's
Pouder box, and a hole passel uv roun pieces uv ivry; but Forrer
ar the rightest way to pernounts it.  I has sence seen the gaim
plaid a sevril number uv times, but kinnot understand it igzackly.

It war a long tiem befo' I cood farly bleeve that Oans he wood
fool me so about the Presydint, and I don't think now he wood
uv dun it ef that ar little yaller fiddlin tacky uv a Melloo hadint a
put him up to it.  I wisht I may be counsoun! ef when I foun
out he had a prinserpul hand in it, ef I didin have a good mine
to war him out aginst the groun.  But, in pint of size, he ain't no
mo' to me then a huckilberry in a wagun, and I nuver yit fit a
runt, and nuver intens to.

Well, I lef the Mintzpi Hous mad is the very devel and distrest in the bargin.  It taint so mighty plesint to find peepul keep
constunt makin fun uv you and deseevin uv you, which shows the
meenniss uv citty folks, which has sense anuf to tend to thar oan
biznis ef they got eny.

I had dun waitid and waitid about that ar skeam uv mine, and
spent munny untel it warnt no use in waitin no longer, and I
coodin bar to wait a minnit mo.  So I goes to my trunk, gits it
out, wrops it up keerfully, and goes and shows it to a man apintid
to tend to them things.  He tole me it warnt wuth a dam.  But I
seen thoo that.  He jes wantid to git me to sell it to him fer
nuthin, then he cood maik a everlastin forchin out'n it.  So I goes
to anuther—thar's hunduds uv um in Washintun, Billy.  He sais

the saim the fust man sed. So I goes to anuther, and anuther, and anuther, untel I wus broke doun with fateeg and dissypintment at the meanniss and jellersy uv mankine. One feller did offer to taik and put it thrue, ef I'd giv him thurty dollars. I'd a giv enything, but when I cum to igsamine my munny pus I foun I didn have five dollars in the worl. This shockt me, cos I knew I owde fer bode and a good meny uther things. The feller offud to taik whut munny I had, but I tole him no, I war blees to keep that, and a gread to giv a writment, a bond, sined with my oan naim. He lafft at me and tole me I wuz a fool. I jes took that thing, wropt it up agin in my hankerchif, went hoam, put it keerfully back in my trunk, and cum back and give that feller the prittiest top-dressin a man uver had. I masht his pleggid nose flat to his roscully fais, and bungd his eyes that bad that I boun he doant see fer six munts. He hollerd murder and the patrollers cum and collard me and carrid me befo a majestrait, and I shood uv hav bin ritin to you in jail, ef Oans and Melloo hadint cum and giv bond and scurety I'd behave myself for a year. They let me go, but I didn keer what becum uv me. I seen the whole worl ware turned aginst me, and when I cum to ask sum cluks which I had lent munny to, I coodin git a cent, and what to do I didn kno. In the eavnin Oans and Melloo tole me Mr. Argruff ware ded, havin blode his brains out with a pistul, and that ar fellar which I had beet fer callin uv me a fool had challindged me to fite him a dewil, intendin to hav my blud. But it warnt so. Mr. Argruff, disgustid at hisself, had packt his trunk and gone . hoam, wharuver that wuz, leavin uv a note advisin uv evryboddy in Washintun to do the saim, cos he sais the devil had done took perseshun uv the sitty, havin uv a bill uv sale fer it in his britchis pockit. And as for that ar feller, I nuver heerd no mo' frum him, sertin.

But my sperits wuz cleen gone, and whotuver wood a becum uv me that nite, the Lord only knows, ef it hadinter bin for Mayan, which her reel naim ain't Mayan a bit, but Noahrer Glennun, a very pritty naim I'm sho, and a better or mo' likely and smarter gearl nuver drord the breth uv life. I coodin stay in the poller uv the Mintzpi Hous, cos all the ladies had got mad with one anuther bout a feller, which I shant call his naim, which wuz a cuttin uv his rusties with all the marrid ladies, and cos anuther man, a membur uv Kongris, which ware a bodin thar, had bin ketched a kissin anuther man's wife in the passige. Then agin, I ware feerd the man whut kep the tarvun (the Mintzpi) wood ass me for the munny I ode him. And in the hous whar I had my room, things wuz orful bad also, cos I ode munny thar too, and ole Swomplans wuz drunk and rarrin around like thunder and wuss, cos he and anuther Kongrissmun had had a quorl. And the Dutchmun and his wife, which had them babis in the room abuv me, had goned away; likewise the railrode man; and Melloo and Oans, they'd gone off; and things wuz dark and desertid tel I farly thought the nex thing Gabrill wood blo' his hon and tiem shood be no mo. And I wure feered to go on the street, becos the rowdis and Plug-Uglis, which had bin behavin bad all the time sense I set foot in the sitty, had dun broke loose and wuz a shootin and a stabbin and a murdrin and a knockin doun and a draggin out everybody that cum along, white or black, rich or po', or enything.

But Noahrer she cum to my room and we had anuther nice, long, confedenshul talk, like we had the nite befo. She ar such a good gearl, Billy, and talks sich good Inglish, and, altho she

knows I aint so mighty smart, pears to rispeckt and look up to
me so.  A man kin no mo help trustin his seekrits to a gearl like
that, than a man kin keep frum warmin himself by a fier when
he's colde.  I tole her about my skeam, who I wuz, whar I cum
frum, my parunts, my little plantashun, niggers, hosses, craps, and
all.  She gimme a heap uv good advise 'bout trustin too much to
peepul, and we all injoyed one nuther's cumpany tell it wuz mighty
nigh 2 o'clock in the mornin agin.  Nuver shill I forgit them two
nites to the longest day I live, and  shill alwais be thankful on account uv wimmin kind in this worl for the saik of Noahrer, fer ef
it hadinter bin fer her, I dunno whethur I shood a bin liftin uv a
pen now, Billy.  Tell Dellywar Sinker to sell evry bit uv the con
and wheet I kin posbly spar and send me the munny drectly,
becos jest is soon is I kin pay off whut I owe, I'm a gointer to
maik that gearl a fust rate present, ef she'll taik it, which I'm
afeerd she wont, seein how high-sprited she ar.

Nex day things took a turn.  Things peered to clear off, like arfter
a long spell uv rain, when Cat Tail ar a risin tremendus, thretnin
to sweep evrything off'n the lo grouns.  Nobody didint dun me
fer no munny, and over at the Mintzpi peepul peared to hav maid
frens, mighty quick I thought, and afars seemed to be workin well
all aroun.  Miss Saludy Trungil and her littil sister didn't giv
themself no grate greef about a losin uv Mr. Argruff, but went
strait ahed, ketchin mo bows, printsply ole men goin to the yung
one, and a ball-hedid gentilmun, with gole spectickles, goin for
Miss Saludy.  They didint plegg me no mo about goin to see the
Presydint at the Forrer Bank, but peared to be pritty mutch wropt
up in thar oan afars.  The bewtiful littil gearl frum Injanner, she
talkt to me sum, and so did them two pritty marrid ladis I tole

you uv. I felt heap bettur. Oans, he cum up and apollygized fer foolin uv me at the Forrer Bank. I tole him that senst he had delivud me out'n the strong arms uv the Lor and the Jestis uv the Pees, I had dun forgiv him long ago. Then he sais:

"To maik up fer my bad conduck, I'll taik you to-night to see the Presydint in fac."

I tole him he coodin fool me no mo; but he sais:

"Thar's a Levvee to-night, and I'll taik you thar, and you can see not only the Presydint and Miss Lain, but all the most distinguisht folks in the kuntry."

It ware a long time befo he and the young ladis helpin uv him could perswade me he warnt a jokin, but finely I kunkloodid to go, and my hoaps uv my skeam revived imeditly. As fer seein uv the Presydint and Miss Lain, whar evrybody wuz, I didint keer so mighty much about it, but I detummind in my oan mine to evale myself uv the okashin to git my projick fairly befo the oanly man in the Yuneyun which wuz likely to do it jestis—vizz: the Presydint. This heer Miss Lain, Billy, her naim are Miss Haryit Lain, and she ar the gneiss (that's the properist way to spell it, Oans says. In fac, Billy, youve notist a gradjul impruvemint in my spellin, which are owin to the fack that Oans and Melloo has been kine enuf to devoat a good eel uv atenshun to me on this pint,) she ar the gneiss uv the Presydint.

Well, cum nite, we-all, that is all the ladis at the Mintzpi, Oans and Melloo and me, got reddy. I wantid to taik Mayan, or ruther Noahrer, along, but she said no. Miss Saludy she wantid I and Oans to go long with her and her par in a hac, but Oans sed we'd better walk. Melloo he went with his sweetarts, which is both the littil Trungil and the pritty littil gal frum Injanner, nobody knows which.

Me and Oans walked on and walked on, way up the Avnew, and hax and carridgis rattlin by us and carryin peepul to the Levvee, untel we past Willud's tavun and the Trezry bildin, a powful manshun, fenst in with pillars in the frunt, whar all the munny uv the Guvnurmint ar put in the seller, which I wisht to goodniss I had about a hundud and fo' dollus uv it just about this tiem, and then we wuz clost to the Igzeckutiv Manshin, as the Presydint's hous ar calld.

Goin along Oans he sais to me, sais he,

" Mozis, a feller goin to the Levvee fer the ferst tiem are gen-rully cunsiderubbly imbarist.  I faintid the ferst tiem I went thar, and Melloo, bein uv a timmid man, took to his bed for 3 weeks arfter-wuds."

S'I, "Dont ef you plees talk that ar way; you skeer me to deth."

S'e, "Not a tall.  I wantid to pepar your mine.  The way fer a feller to do, ar jest to act igzactly at his ees, maik himself puffickly at hoam, cos the hous don't blong to the Presydint, but to the peepul of the Yunited Staits, which givs it to him, chargin uv him no rent, and you bein one uv the peepul uv the Yunitid Staits, uv coas it belongs to you much as to enybody elts.  You ar jest is good is enybody, and you must act a kordin."

I tole him I ware much ableeged to him fer tellin uv me, ptickly that part about the hous blongin to me, and which tharfo I shood feel intily and puffickly at hoam.

We went on, passin by a heap uv hax and things, goin thoo a iun gate, long a kervd pavemint whar thar wuz mo' hax strung out in a lien and mo' a comin constunt, untel we got to the White Hous, which ar anuther naim for the Igzeckutiv Manshin. It have a imments big poche in frunt uv it, like the poche uv a Kote Hous, with very tall pillows, and, kuyus enuf, the hax and carridgis drives right spang into this poche, and one half uv it havin no flo at all but a gravly rode runnin rite thoo it, and the uther half bein paved with rock, and hisetid abuv the groun that you has to go up a few steps to git to it.

Uv the glowry and the splendur, the menny peepul and the bar-armd and barneckt ladies I seen inside, wurds, Billy, kin giv you no idee, not the leest. I ruther think it beets the Forrer Bank and the Ixchain both put together. A white sarvunt, look to me like a Prisbyteyun preechur, took our hats and big coats soon's we got in, giv us a brass check fer um like they givs fer your trunk on the railrode, and jobbed them in a hole, which they had about a thousun holes made thar for the puppus.

Me and Oans then smoothed our hars and pepard to git interjuist to the Presydint. I nuver felt mo nachrul in my life, and wuz rezolootly rezolvd to hav my skeam atentid to that very nite. In order to git to the Presydint you has to go throo about twenty diffrent rooms, all openin into one anuther, all uv a diffrint culler, blue and red and green and white, and full uv the most magniffysent fernicher, gilt mostly with gold, and shinin under the gas light tel it farly addles your brane. The peepul thats goin to be interjuist to the Presydint forms in a line, two and two, like mustrin, and, arm in arm, goes on frum one room to anuther untel at last they git to the one whar the ole man stands up and shakes hands with evrybody. Oans ketcht me by the arm, and we went on and on and on mighty slow, peepul, bar-neckt ladis printsply, befo us,

and peepul behind us, and the ferst thing I know, thar wuz the
Presydint—a powful, hevvy-bilt, tall, ole, greyhedid man, with a
white crevat, his hed twisted one side, and his eye ruther cockt.
Oans ware interjuist ferst, and then a man that stood thar fer the
ixpress purpus, grabbed me by the elbow, and assed me my naim;
I tole him Mozis Addums, and he sais "Mister Mozis Addums,
Mister Presydint; Mister Presydint, Mister Mozis Addums," and
the Presydint shook me, ruther keerlessly I thought, by the hand,
and moved it, kinder pushin me off frum him.  But I ware bent
apun seein uv him about that thing, so I sais in a very klectid and
oddibul vois, so is to show peepul like I ware used to bein thar,
and felt at hoam in my oan hous—I sais, "Kin I see you a minnit,
Mr. Cannun?  Jes' step this way, ef you pleas."

He jukt his hand away, and begins a shakin hands with sumbody behine me, pretendin like he didint heer me, which I knowd
he did, cos thar wuz a genrul movemint all round, like sumthin
had hapind.  I muss say I considud this as bein desididly bad
mannurs.  He may be a very grate man, but I and uther peepil
hires him by the ear to ten to our bizness, and twuz is littil as he
cood do to treat a body rispecktfully.

Enny way I had to leeve him.  Lookin roun fer Oans, I coodin
see him, and I sais, "Whar's Oans?" and nobody anserd, and
anuther man ketcht me by the elbo agin, and interjuisis me to
Miss Lain, the gneiss uv the ole Presydint.  She ware a splendid
lookin lady, drest in black (Oans tole me, arfterwuds, she wuz in
monin fer Mr. Lecompting) and havin uv her arms and shoalders
bar, and havin, I swar, uv the finist skin I uver see, white is satin.
I warnt discumboberated nun, but remembrin I wuz in my oan
hous, sais;

"Good eavnin', Miss Haryit; I'm glad to see you lookin so well this eavnin. Tollibul nise cumpny you got heer this eavnin. Ruther warm for the timer year."

She made me a low curchy, and she said to me:

"I thanky, Sir," she sais, "I'm only tollibul this eavnin," and then she wuz goin to say sumthin mo' but wuz took with a fit uv coffin behine her fan, and stopt.

S'I, "You got mighty pritty har, Miss Haryit. You remines me a good eel uv my cussin Betsy Flatback, only she's a dark-skinned gearl, and you aint got no bumps on your forrud, nar a one, is fer as I kin see."

I thought I heern a kine uv tittrin and gigglin a goin on all aroun me, which I reckin I did heer it, and which I has no doubt wuz on account uv po Oans, which jest at that minnit ketcht me and hauled me away, rite throo the croud, which apeard to be a cunsiderbul disturbid, is well is myself, fer his saik. I nuver did see such a fais as po Oans had. Lookt like it ware goin to bust plum opin, it ware so red and so full uv blud. He cum as nigh having uv a aperplecksy and cunvulshins is enny man I uver see to miss it. He coodin speak a word, but hauled me along arfter him, way out uv the croud, I a thinking he wuz goin hoam, cos he wuz turribly sick at his stummuck. But he carrid me to the eend uv a long passige, whar thar wuz a big glass hous, full uv trees, and the minnit he got thar, he laid down among the tubbs whar the trees wuz plantid in, and rolld over and over like he wuz a gointer die evry secund. I war goin fer a doctur, but he woodint let me. And he made the kuyusist soun, like laffin, and when I see his fais, it lookt like he ware laffin, but fit to kill his-self with it.

S'I, "Mr. Oans, you laffin, aint you?"

But his jaw were lockt, and he rolled over and skuffild aroun the tubbs wuss then ever. I knowd he ware in agny, but it sounded so much like laffin I ware bleest to ask him agin:

"But *aint* you laffin, Mr. Oans?"

It ware a long tiem befo he cood reply, and when he did, he fetcht breath so hard it ware misry to heer him. He sais:

"Oh! Lord, no. I'm not a laffin. I've got a aperplectic fit. My famly is subjick to um, and when they has um, nobody skeersly kin bleeve they aint laffin."

And he laid thar pantin, like a houn arfter a long chase. I reckin it wuz nigh unto a nour befo he sufishintly rekuvered to git up and go back whar the cumpny wuz. I bresht his clothes, which they wuz full uv dirt whar he had rolld on the flo' uv the glass hous, and we went back. But, po feller! he hickupt and gobbled fer breth and his eyes run water so, that evrybody kep a lookin at me and him saim like we wuz a cupple uv wild anemils, makin it very onplesant to be thar. So when we cum acrost Miss Saludy Trungil and sum uther folks frum the Mintzpi Hous, which they seemed to hav heerd how bad off Oans he wuz, and he tole Miss Saludy he ware so week he cood barly stand, she offerd him a seet in her carridge, and we giv our chex and got our hats and coats, put um on, and cum back, most uv the uther Mintzpi folks folrin behine us in thar hax. I warnt sorry to leav the seen uv so mutch splendur, becos the cheef objick uv my visit, that is, seein uv the Presydint about my skeam, ware knockt on the hed. Comin back, Oans ware took so bad agin with his cunvulshins, he ware foast to leen his hed on Miss Saludy's shoalder, and cried and lafft and gobbled thar like a chile. She ware mighty good to him, and took him rite into the poller uv the Mintzpi; and thar I left him and her and Melloo, and neerly all the rest uv um, being ankshus myself to git over to my room, becos I felt ruther badly.

I hadin hardly got down the steps uv the Mintzpi, befo I heerd the most orful laffin in the worl in the poller. And thar wuz po Oans, neerly ded with a fit uv aperplecksy. I do think sitty folks is the most unfeelin uv humin beans.

Tell um to fix up evrything at hoam, fer I'm a cummin the minnit I pay my debts. I aint goin to stay in this durn plais no longer.

Yose truly,

MOZIS ADDUMS.

## EIGHTH LETTER.

POOR MOZIS! NO MUNNY. COMPLEAT FAILURE OF HIS SKEAM.
AN IXPLQSHUN. BEDSIDE SEENS. ROW AT MOZIS'S WEDDING.
BRILYUNT REALIZASHUN OF HIS SKEAM. THE EEND.

DEAR BILLY:

Billy, why in the worl diden you send that ar
munny on suner? You mighter saved me a monsus site of
trubil. I tell you I've been throo the rubbus sence I last writ,
and has seen a worl uv oneezyness uv mine, and bin nighly ded,
body and sole.

I watid and watid to heer from you. I kep axin the post-
master about yo letter tel he got rite mad with me, and ef he
hadenter lived in sech a big, nise, rock hous, and bin pertecktid
behine such a tremendus winder with only heer an thar a hole in
it—ef it hadenter bin for this, I and he wouler got into a fite sertin, becos I ware madder longer him than he ware mad longer me.
But nar letter nuver cum, and I kep on gittin mo' miserbler and
mo' miserbler evry day, tel I thought I'd giv the gose rite strait
up then and thar, and nuver see you all and ole Ferginny agin
fum tiem tel eternity. Winter had dun goned, but spring, which
put forth her leaves uv green an her grass uv green und her small
berds whitch sings in the tops uv the trees,—spring fetched no
comfut to po' Mozis, owin, I jedged, mainly to the fact uv the
9

want uv munny, a change uv arr, and turnup sallet, which has
a fine efec on my livur.   In deede, the joyusness uv Nacher
seemed fer to mawk my stait uv feelins, and the singing uv the
birds and the laffin uv the gearls at the Mintzpi Hous, whitch they
wuz boun to keap up with the ceezin, havin uv thar neks and
armes barer than uver—these heer apeard speshully to damp my
sperits that bad that no licker nor whiskey nor nuthin dun um
eny good.                                                    .

Then agin, Tormint lookt like it had bust apun the accussid
sitty.   Newmerus Kongrismen and ofisers uv the Army and
uthers had had fites and kep on havin mo uv um, and leckshun
tiems a cummin on in the sitty sturd up the biel uv the rowdis tel
a inchsreckshun uv niggers ware but a privit wrassil cumpard to
um.   Evry nite, *evry* singal nite and in the day too, rite on the
mainist street, sumbody ware kild, shot, stobd, knockt in the hed,
and sumtimes haf a duzen at a tiem wuz slayd in cole blud.

Oans tole me is menny is 2 hundud wuz throte-cut in 1 day,
but this ware a speshees uv igzadjurashun whitch subsurves no
good puppus ixcep to friten a man and gits tisum arfter a tiem.
He sed he carrid 8 revolters and 2 booy nives on his pussun
whenuver he went out in the street, and edvised me to do the
saim, but I diden hav nuthin to buy no weepuns with, whitch
tellin him, he gose and bize me a bigg gunn loadened with gravil
and tacks, but I got erestid the ferst day I shoaldud it, and he
had to git me outn the hands of the Jestis uv the Pees agin, arfter
whitch he got me a hoss pistul, whitch he maid me carry it doun
my back in tween my shoalder blaids to keep from bein ubservd,
tharby givin me uv a heap uv inkunveenyunts, owing to the thing
droppin konstuntly doun into my britches, twel I had to tie the

butt eend uv it with a twien string, which I hilt in my han all the tiem, and then I felt free to fase a frounin worl uv all the Plug Uglis in kreashin.

Thar wuz I amewsment that it might have consold me, but fer I thing. The Captul yard and the Presydint's yard bein all green and the weather bein plezint uv a evenin, a big ban uv mewzishiners, drest in red cotes like the British, whitch it ar calld the Mreen Ban, yust to cum wunst or twiest a week and play to hunduds and thousins uv peepul that flockt to heer um, awl the bewty and the shiverulry uv the sitty bein thar, prantzin and pradin and shoin off thar fine clothes, and little gals in short frocks and hoops runnin up and doun, up and doun, lively as crickits, and evry thing gay is it possbly cood be. But I diden injoy it nun. Mayan warnt thar, and then agin I ware thinkin uv my skeem, hoam, dets, and a heap uv trubilsum things.

One evenin when the Ban ware playin at the Presydint's grounds, I lookt over the wall and thar, on a littil hill, set a passel uv Injuns, squottid doun on sum rock, smokin thar pipes, watchin the fashenubil croud, and thinkin uv thar oan thots. It ware a moanful site to see, Billy—when a feller remembud that wunst apun a tiem all the grate sitty uv Washintun yewst to blong to them Injuns' 4-farthers, and now nar one uv um oand anuf lan thar to dig um a graive. Me and them apeard to be like wun anuther fer retchidness. They had loss thar pozeshuns and I had dun loss my hoaps. They wuz fer, fer away fum hoam, and so wuz I. They had no frens, and I had no munny, and I ware goin to say frens nuther, but I wont say that. And thar the bewtyfull musick played and the pritty ladis and the hansum gintilmen and the happy childun walkt to the soun uv it, and thar wuz me and

them po Injuns lookin moanfully on, hevy-hartid anuf, Billy, and
too hevy—feelin we had no rite to be whar soe mutch injoymint
ware goin on, and nuthin, nuthin to look forrard to. I cood a cryd
thinkin about it, and went away sorrerfull—both fer myself and
them po Injuns.

But what wust a flictid me and jobbd me doun into the very
gulp up dispar, wer not so mutch the want uv munny an bein
away from hoam and all that, but this, Billy. Wun day, that
ar ball-heded ole gentilmin whitch I tole you ware the bo uv Miss
Saludy Trungil, and whitch he wars them gole specks I menshind,
—wun day, he cum to me, and havin heerd, I nuver cood tell how,
about my skeam, entud into convusashin with me about it. After
a good eel uv persuashin I jes candidly tole him all the whole
bizniss frum beginnin to een, and eaven took and showd him the
thing itself. He keerfully lookt at it, and sed it showd a oncum-
mun amount uv tallent indeed, but then he shuk his ball-hed, and
makin me go to his apartmint, whar he had a reeul liberry uv
books a layin on the flo', and, takin out wun uv the largist vol-
yums, red me the histry uv the subjick, whitch it apears, so fur
frum bein aridganul with me, hav ockyupide the mines uv men
frum the tiem uv Tuber Kane to the presint day. Then he ixplained and pruved to me how, in the very nacher uv things, the
skeam ware impossabul and nuver, *nuver* cood be dun by nobody
on top of the erth, I diden keer how smart and edjukatid they
wuz. He shorely are a kine and sensabul ole gentilmun, and sich
I tole him, tho' my hart ware fit to brake at the very momint. He
sed that thousuns uv peepul had cum to Washintun on the saim
bizness pecisely, and he had seen wun uv um, a miserbul blind man
frum Kaintucky, the day befo. He istablisht to my inti satisfack-

shun that the mo' a man thinks uv this heer kind uv a skeam the
wuss it ar fer him, and ef he keeps on he ar certin to go distracktid.

I hilt out is long is I cood, but finely I was bleest to cave in.
So, Billy, all my vizyuns uv welth and happaniss wuz teetotuly
smasht feruver and feruver mo. I had nuthin to do but go back
hoam and skratch the saim po' man's back whar I had alwais
skratched. Thar wuz no help fer it, nun, not the leetlist teenchy
bit uv a shadder uv it. It ware a mortil blow. It hert me mo'
than the tiem you all cut doun the sickamo whar I was up tryin to
git a kewn outen his holler, and ef I had'nt bin flung in the lap
uv the tree when it falled, I'd a bin killd beyond redempshun.
You reckolect I ware ded any way fer haf a day.

All ware certny over now. Mozis, po' creetur, had cum to
Washintun, maid a fool uv himself, spent all his munny and mo'
besides, coodin git away, and the whole erth wuz black befo him
is the back uv a chimbly. It ware a tiem what tride men's soles.
It wuz dubbil and twistid mizry and wo. I hoap and pray you'll
nuver git in no sitch trubbil, nor enny boddy elts, ixcept it wuz
the meanist man that uver lived.

Havin givin up all idee uv my skeam, hatin uv it in fac, I tuk
the thing outen my trunk and flinged it outen the winder, but
Noahrer, is I arfterwoods foun, gethered it up and saved it for
herself. But what she wantid with it I dunno. She did her very
bess to keep my sperits up, but I ware in the lo grouns uv sorrer
and coodint git outen um all I and she cood doo. But I shill
alwais luv her fer it. Wimmin, Billy, is the All-heelin Intmint uv
the worl; ef it twarnt for them we men fokes wood all hav long
sence departid this life with ring-wurrum uv the sole, and gone to

the land uv shaddus, scabby all over our harts, with the 7 ear
eetch broke out so bad that no amount uv brimstone doun belo
cood uver cure us.

Driv to desprashun by cummin out at the little eend uv the
ho'n with my skeam, I maid the most ankshus inkwiris arfter
munny, tryin fer to borry sum uv it. Then, fer the ferst tiem, I cum
to a nollidge uv the fac that the whole toun uv Washintun are
broke all to peecis, sold in a deed uv truss, bankrup intily. Oans
sed he diden hav no munny, sed Melloo diden hav nun, Argruff
ware goned away, sed nobody diden have nun, ixcep it twuz sum
men whar makes a livin by lendin uv it at 20 per sent a munth.
Its the plain truth, Billy, that thar's men in Washintun which
spends thar lives in ruinin the po clucks, lendin um munny at
enawmus intruss, manidjin so that they keep konstunt payin and
nuver do pay out, bullyin uv um too in the most shameful manner. I tell you, ef the haf I heers is the trooth, these here men
is devils incarnit, and one uv um in pticler is sitch a cole-bludid,
remawsless, diabollikle, infunnil, konfoundid ole villin uv a feen
that it wood giv me unaloid plezure to menshin his naim and
ixpose him to the papers and to the skorn and indignashun uv
mankine. It orter be dun, and sumbody will do it sum uv these
dais, and then I do hoap and pray that the peepul will jes taik
him and all that's like him and burn um to ashes in the publick
squarr. It woodin be no mo then what they desurves, and it
wood be a treatin uv um a heap kinder than they has treetid the
po clucks for yeers and yeers.

That this sort uv a thing shood be countnunst in a Cristchun
land ar sumthin I kinnot acount for. The fac that hunduds and
hunduds uv abil bodid yung men (sum uv um is old and weak

tho,) shood let this thing run on without makin eny atemp to put a stop to it, shud let a few rich ole devils rule um with a rod uv iun—this fac shose the abjec sperit, and chickin-hartid sort uv men whar lives in toun. Stay at hoam, Billy, whar you kin be free, and frade uv nuthin that draws the breth uv life.

But what wuz cuyus and unakountibul to me, ware the suckumunts folrin—that the very thing that disturbid my mine and which it made me so eegur to borry munny, were the very thing that nuver happind to me. I ode for bode and for room rent and washin and uther things to vayus and sundre peepul. I ode um, and, coz yew diden sen the munny, kep on a owin um mo en mo, and nar one uv um dund me. Day arfter day, I kep on ixpectin uv um to do it. Thinx I, to-day I'll ketch it sertin, and whut to say I dunno. But they diden do it—*they nuver did dun me wunst.* Warnt this straindge? It skeerd me; I diden know what to maik uv it. Tellin Oans about it, it alomd him too. He remarked, he sais the like uv it nuver had happind in Washintun fum the foundashin uv the sitty. Melloo sed sumthin ware rottin in Denmok, sertin. But nun uv us kood akount for it, and yo letter not a cummin, me and the postmarster kep on a quarlin thro the hole in his winder, (I had a good mine to job a stick in his drottid eye fer him.) So I jes went long, leevin things to Provydents pritty mutch.

Endurin uv thees miserabul dais, I walkt and walkt and walkt, awl the tiem, to cam my mine ef posbil and git shed uv the site uv so menny peepul, whitch the site uv um maid me mad is fier. In fac evry thing frettid and distrest me. I diden have no pease day nor nite, nowhar, nor with enybody, unlest it wuz Noahrer, whitch I liked her better and more betterer evry day. I walkt

doun to a plase they calls the Knavy Yard, and seen the kannuns
and the kannun balls by the milyuns, and the ships and things,
but it dun me no good.  I seen um makin uv brass nails thar
faster then you kin shell pees, but it jes' frettid me.  I went to a
plais naimd Jawdge Toun, a damdabul horrid plals as uver wuz
bilt apun top the groun, quiut is the graive and derty is a hog
pen, and bein thar maid me feel like I had the pawlzy.  I wundud
how humins cood live thar.  I went to sevril berryin grouns, but
the toomstoans urrytatid me.

When uver I walkt about I carrid ·my hoss pistul doun my
back, reddy and willin to incownter the Devil, and all his gang uv
rowdis whitch they ar calld Rams, ef nesesery, becoz I felt like
fiten all the tiem, and evry body.  But no body diden pester me
nun ixcep twuz beggers, whitch jest is sune is I had dun spent
every singul solitery sent I had in kreashun, begun to cum rite
arfter me, consoun thar dirty soles!  I giv um a pees uv my mine
pritty planely, but they diden seem to hav no memry, but kontinyud arfter me evry day uv the worl (Miss Saludy sais Oans
and Melloo imploid um to do it, but taint so,) makin uv me so
fuyus twuz mutch is I cood do to keep frum blowin thar mis-
erubul ole branes outen that good for nuthin ole heds uv um,
plaig taik um! ding um!

My favrit walk, tho, ware doun to the rivur at the warf whar
the steem botes cum that cum frum ole Ferjinny.  I ust to go
thar and set and think how happy the day wood be when I cum
to go hoam agin, and thar I'd immadjin myself goin back so eesy,
ferst on the Orindge rode to Ritchmun, then the Damdvile, then
the Sowthside to Fomvil, and frum thar to Kerdsvil, and then rite
smac hoam—it seemd like nuthin.  But when I kum to remem-

ber I diden hav a cent, then it ware impossybul, intily so, and I mite is well hav bin in the Mune for eny chants thar wuz to git back. It cumfittid me rite smart tho to set thar and look and look twards hoam for hours at a tiem, and ef it haden bin for the Washintun Monumint whitch it seemd to bee konstunt wotchin me, I shood mity nigh hav injoied myself thar.

One mornin I went doun thar rite erly and set way out on the back part uv a ole steem bote whar nobody cooden see me and ass me no questchuns. It ware a powful cool day for the tiem uv year, makin uv me mo' mellunkolly then I uver had been in awl my life. Peard to me like my tiem had cum, and I diden keer ef it had. I thot about you all, Billy. "Ef I has ar a fren in the worl," I sais to myself, "it ar Billy Ivvins. But he aint rote to me, and he aint goin to. I reckin they reckin I'm ded, and I wisht too grashus I wuz. I'd better be ded than suffer whut I has induode." I fergivd yew all, Billy, but my hart wuz sick, mighty sick. The sun went under the klowds and stade thar, and the wind blowd cold is ice, chillin me to the very marro. I hoped it wood freize me ded. But thar I sot, watchin the miserbul river that looked so cold and so much uv it, movin up and doun, up and doun, all the tiem, like the brest uv a man with the knew-mony or ploorisy fetchin his breth short. So the cold rivur kep breethin, like it ware in trubbil, had seen a heep uv trubbil and mo wuz a cummin. And then, way, way off yondur, whar hevvin and earth cum together, it lookt dark and shet up, like a hous whar the peepul haden jes gone to cherch and wuz cummin back bime by, but had gone for good and all. It ware mo' than I cood bar, Billy. I drapt my hed, not cryin, but groanin in the groans uv unbarabul agny uv spirit.

It wuz cleen dark befo I lookt up agin.    I diden want to go back to toun; but I diden wanter stay.    So I walks mecannykly along, seein and heerin uv nuthin, ropt in my own miserbul feelins.    Presintly I heers a loud holrin and sees a brite lite, and, lookin, I sees about two hundid rowdis gethered roun a barl uv tarr, a burnin in a opin plais.    One uv um hollers at me, " Hello, you dam Plugg, whar you goin ?"    It sot me on fier at wunst—it ware the very thing I wantid.

"Cum on!" I sais, "cum on! you villins, I dont keer how menny.    You aint a goin to run over me, sertin.    Cum on; I be dad shimd ef I doant maik roscul branes cheep in Washintun is oshturs."

Sho nuf, they cum a runnin and holrin like they wuz goin to eet me rite up.    But I ware prepard for um tho.    My hoss-pistul had dun slipt way doun, but I foun the string, and wuz a drawin uv her keerfully up ; when they got so clost to me, I give a hard jirk, and thar ware a ixploshun like sumbody had blastid the rock uv Gibrawltur and the Blewridje wide opin, and I knode no mo. In the words uv the poitry,

> Silunts, like a Pole, tis cum',
> Toe heel the bloze uv soun.

When I cumd too, I wuz a layin in my oan bed in my oan room and the room ware full of kumpny.    Things all lookt like thees heer insides uv thees heer glass balls they has on parler tabils, and peerd like my sentsis wuz outen my hed and a settin on top uv the hed uv the bed, a lookin doun at my oan self like I ware sumbody elts in glass, is well is the rest uv the cumpny. Thar wuz Oans und Melloo, Miss Saludy and her sister, the luvly littel Injanner gearl, the two bewtiful marrid ladis, and the ole ball-hedid ole gentilmun—all a lookin at me. And Noahrer she set rite at the side uv my bed.

"How pail he is," sais one uv the ladis.

"No wundir," sais Oans, "arfter him a losin ate galluns uv blud."

"Po feller!" sais the ladis.

"Reckin he'll die?" sais the littil Trungil.

"Die!" sais Melloo, "not a bit uv it. He's sich a good, simpil mindid anemil, he dont know how to die. You'd hav to giv him a set uv printid instruckshins, with a small map uv the rout and evin then, ten chancis to one, he'd git lost. You'd hav to do is they do in my country—send a boy with him to show him the way."

"You orter be ashamed to talk that a way," sais littil Injanner.

"Well," he sais, "I will be, ef you say so."

"In fac," sais Oans, "he's in grait dainjur."

"Hiesh!" sais the far-har'd marrid lady, "he knows what you talkin' 'bout."

"No he don't," replize Oans, "he's lookt jest that a way for the last week, but intly outen his hed."

"Git up frum thar, gearl," sais Miss Saludy, "and lemme smooth his piller."

I see Noahrer's eye flash fier and the culler cum crimsun to her cheek, but she anserd very perlitely:

"His piller is nise anuf, Miss, and the Docther sais he musnt be dishtubd, Miss," she sais.

"I do bleeve the gearl's in luv with Mozis," sais Miss Saludy to one of the ladis.

"Its a spakin for yeself, ye ar Miss," ansers Noahrer, very sharp.

And then, Billy, evrything faded away agin.

The nex thing I remembers, it was nite, and no candil in the room, only a feebil lite cummin frum the stoav. Sumbody ware talkin rite clost to me.

"Poor, poor boy! So fur away frum hoam. No farther ner mother nor bruthers nor sisters; all aloan heer in this grate sitty, and nun but a servunt gearl to watch over him. The good Lord keep gard over him, and pertect him and saiv him."

It ware Noahrer, Billy, and she wuz a cryin. She bent over and kist me. I sais nuthin, but I thot thots. Then she went off a littil ways and kneeld doun by a cheer—she wuz a prayin for me. I laid rite still, but the teers run like rain, soft teers that cum eesy and plentiful and dun me good to cry um. I nuver knowd befo that enybody cood cry them kind uv teers, which wuz so plesint and relievin.

A good meny uther pityful things happind in this way, Billy, when nobody didn't bleeve I had enny idee uv what ware goin on, fer I wuz that weak I didn't keer evin to move, mutch mo speek.

How I cum to be in this deplobul condishin, Oans arfterwuds told me. He's got him a unkil that livs in the sitty, a ole gentilmun uv onhappy sperits but havin uv a kine warm hart, and this heer unkil wuz a goin hoam the nite I met them rowdis burnin uv the tar barl, and foun me, and had me took hoam, mo' ded then alive. I jedge the hoss pistul, which Oans had loadened it to the muzzil with brass tax, went off when I jerkt it—bustid all to flinders, cuttin opin a bigg vahe in my hed or neck, and mighty nigh killin uv me. When I ware foun, nuthin ware lef uv the hind part of my cloaths, sais Oans, but my kote koller and the heels uv my boots, and them had bin on fier, but got put out with my oan blood. His unkil are uv opinyun that sum uv the rowdis must uv sufurd is well is myself, thar bein a good eal uv loose flesh layin aroun, which, fer a marikle, nun uv it cum frum me, tho I wuz scorcht horribil.

I wont giv you no mo pticklers tel I see you, which, thank the Lord, will be in a feu dais frum this tiem. Neethur will I tell you how Noahrer wotcht and nusst me the whole tiem like I had bin her farther, or her bruther, or a little chile uv her oan, hirin uv anuther gearl her oan self to tend to the hous. Ef she hadent bin pritty, ef she hadint bin smart, I'd a bin bleest to luv her for this. But what techt me deepist, ware, when I got well and she giv me yo letter havin uv the munny in it. Oans hapnin to cum in about that tiem, I told him secritly, for I diden want Noahrer to put herself to no mo trubel about me, to tell the lanlod uv the Mintzpie to cum heer I wantid to see him. So he cum and I handid him the munny, makin no apolligy for not payin him befo, becos I ware too weak to talk much.

"Why, haow's this," he sais, talkin Yankee, "I guess ye dont owe me northin. I calclate yere rite squar up tew the day. You sent me sum munny by that gurl yistiddy."

Noahrer run outen the room.

"Well," he sais, "goodby. I got no time to chat. Hope you'll be out in a few days," and away he went like a steem injine, is he is.

When the truth cum out, which it diden cum eesy, becos she tride to lay it on sumbody elts, but it ware boun to cum sooner

10

or later, I found that Noahrer had took the munny her Pa sent her to cum hoam to Ireland on, and had paid my bode, my room rent, my washin and all with it, spendin uv nigh unto a hundud dollers and a most every cent she had, for me.

My mine were made up arfter this, ef it hadint bin befo. Soon is I got well enuf to walk bout my room pritty strong, I gethurd all my energis fer the effut, but the minnit I got to the pint to speek the cole chills and pusprashin broke out and I had to say nuthin. Fo' or fiev tiems this acurd, tel at last I got rite mad with myself fer bein uv sich a cowud, and befo I knowd it I sais out loud:

"Noahrer!"

And I sed it so feerse she jumpt up frum whar she wuz a settin sewin, not knowin what to maik uv it. I ware standin up too. I told her I ment enything elts but to speek to her harshly, and then ketchin holt uv both her nise plump, littil hands, I sed—I dunno whut I sed—I koted her, trimblin all the tiem tel I coud hardly stand up. She ware bleest to see I ware in erniss, and then she cummenst a trimblin too. Her culler cum and went like fier tryin to ketch—she hung back like a gate with a bad fall—but when she cum, I tell you she cum. That gate slatcht too like it ware nuver goin to be opin'd no mo foruver. I must uv hav kist her a thousing uv tiems.

Billy, thar's barm in Gilyud, Billy—thar's a fezeeshun thar, surtin. The docktur frum that deestric hav bin practisin on me for mo'n a week, and I'm a mendin rapidly. Git yo Ma and cussin Fanny to go over to my hous and maik the folks cleen up is cleen is cleen kin be. I and Noahrer is a cummin shortly. I forgivs myself for her saik for cummin heer to Washintun with

my pleggid skeem, but I shell be consoundid glad to git back to
ole Buckingame and breeth the ar rite fresh frum Willis's mountin
wunst mo.

We wuz marrid a few days ago, marrid in cherch, not by no
Cathlic but by a reglur Baptiss, Noahrer sayin she'd do enything
to plees me, and as fer relidgin, she'd alwais bin a Protestunt, altho' she went to the Cathlic cherch.  A lardge cumpny uv ladis
and gentilmen frum the Mintzpi cum to atend the serremony, but
Oans, which I had ptickly countid apun him, ickskewsed himself
on acount uv bizniss, he bein uv a cluk, you know.  The marridge wuz a goin on very nise, altho' I ware rite smartly skeered
and weak in the knees, when I heers a turbul fuss behine me, and
the nex thing sumbody had dun collard me.  Turnin roun, I seen
a big ole gentilmun, mighty red in the fais, holdin me by the
collar, shakin a gole-heddid kain at my nose, and holrin in a
most powful vois:

"I ferbid the serrymony!  I ferbid it.  He shell not marry my
dawter.  You villin," he sais to me, "I've caught you.  I'll teech
you, you scoundrul, to run away with a gentlemun's dawter.
Take that, you roscul!" and he bungd me on the nose with the
gole hed uv his kain.

The ladis screemed feerful, and little ole Melloo hollerd out,
"it's a mistaik, a mistaik, this aint you dawter, sir."  But I knowd
he ware Noahrer's farther, which had crost the sea arfter her, but
I didn't keer whose farther he wuz, he shoodint hit me; so I
drord off, and I ware is mad is the devil, and spanged him rite in
the middle uv the forrud and laid him cole.  Nuver wuz thar sich
a fuss uv screemin and holrin—holrin fur the pleece, which they
didint cum a tall.

Noahrer run to her farther, whar he wuz a layin flat uv his back on the flo, to atend to him, but she hadint farly techt him befo she bounct up with her fais full uv the most intents disgust. Twarnt no farther uv hern, twarnt no farther uv nobody, it ware Oans— a consoundid villin uv a roscul! which had gone and drest up in ole Kongrismun Swomplans' cloathes, buttnin uv a pillar in his breeches fer fatt, borryin his gole-heddid kain, and a paintin uv his fais red to maik out he ware mad, and cummin playin that fool trick on me and Noahrer! I wer feerd I had kilt him, but he cum to his sensis arfter a while, and wuz well anuf to be at the party they giv us that night at the Mintzpi, tho' he had a bump on his forrud, which it made him look like a yung eunuchorn, Miss Saludy sed.

His horn in his forrud, and my bungd nose, made um all laff mightly, and we injoyed the evenin perdidjus. Noahrer wuz alowed by all but the ladis to be the prittiest and smartist lady thar, the gentilmen all fallin in love with her, which made me feal prowd as I dunno whut. Ole Swomplans swo he wuz goin to kill me fer my widder, but he ware jest a joakin.

After Oans wuz carrid outen the cherch, the marridje serremony perseedid nisely to the very eend—we wuz made tite and fast in the wholly bons of matrimony, which it rejoyst my heart ixseedingly. When the cumpny all got out and had dun got in thar hax, and Noahrer in hern, and I jest about to follow her, Melloo ketcht me by the arm and took me one side, sayin:

"Lemme congratulate you."

"Sertny," I sais, "jest is much is you pleese."

"I don't mean about your marridge, but your skeam," he sais.

S'I, "Drot the skeam! I nuver want to heer it menshind."

"Whut!" he sais, "not arfter so brillyunt a realizashin uv it?"
I told him I did'n understand him—no mo' I didnt.

S'e, "Hav you lookt at your wife keerfully?"

"Well," I sais, "not ptickly as yit."

"I mean her fais," he sais.

"Sertny," I sais, "I kist her wunst."

"Did you notice enything pecuelyer about her fais?" he sais.

S'I, "Nuthin, ixcept it twuz mighty pritty and good."

"Well," he sais, "unless she diffurs very grately frum eny woman I uver saw, or uver herd uv, you will, if you igzamine keerfully, find sumwhar between the nose and chin a importunt apperchur."

"A apperchur," I sais.

"Yes," he sais, "a openin."

"Her mouth," I ixclaims.

"Igzackly," he sais, "and tharin lies the compleat foolfillmunt uv yo skeam."

"S'I, "Goodness knows! whut do you mean?"

Sais he, "Tharin, that is, in that thar apperchur or openin, or mouth, and in that thar openin aloan uv all places in this world, you will find PERPETCHUL MOSHUN!"

> In haist tel we meet,
>> Yo ole frend,
>>> MOZIS ADDUMS.

# NOTES.

FIRST LETTER, *Page 11.*—"Gon." Gongs, once so common in all the large hotels, have gone so completely out of fashion that, in reading this letter in public, I have observed that the younger members of the audience failed entirely to understand me, and of course could not appreciate Addums's fright at first hearing one.

*Page 14.*—The American Hotel of that day was on the corner of Main and Eleventh streets, where Levy's great dry goods store now stands, and was kept, I believe, by Mr. Duval, or, possibly, by Mildeburger Smith.

*Page 16.*—If I remember rightly, the bronzes of Henry and Jefferson were placed first upon the "banisters," as Mozis called them, of the steps at the western entrance to the Capitol, and the equestrian statue of Washington lay for some time in a huge box tilted up against the present monument.

SECOND LETTER, *Page 22.*—More than twenty years have passed since Addums first saw the Washington Monument in Washington city, yet it stands now precisely as it stood then, unfinished—a reflection and a disgrace upon the American people.

*Page 25.*—Addums evidently mistook the clerk (Stewart was his name, I think) for Mr. Brown. The furniture in some of the rooms at Brown's was at that time antiquated to a degree, but has long since given place to more modern, but not, on that account, more comfortable, styles.

*Page 27.*—"Argruff" was suggested by an unfortunate young gentleman from the South, who died, I believe, soon after Addums left the city.

*Page 31.*—The picture of boarding house keepers is exaggerated, but not greatly so. Some very unhappy specimens were to be seen in Washington in Mozis's day, and may be now, for aught I know to the contrary.

THIRD LETTER, *Page 34.*—The mysterious "sine bode" was simply a sign of some restaurant that had failed and was placed away in a garret into which Addums from his back window often peered.

*Page 35.*—"Swomplans" was in fact only a clerk to a member of Congress.

*Page 43.*—The Democratic party before the war being divided on the question of Slavery in the Territories, it was ingeniously argued that this division of sentiment gave the party additional strength, enabling it to carry both sections— a puzzle to more people than Mozis.

FOURTH LETTER, *Page 45.*—"Dekade colluds." This is a slander. The eating at the "Mintzpi" was quite good, except as to corn bread—that is never good north of Virginia, unless it be in parts of Maryland.

*Page 47.*—Among the many ladies at the above hotel, one of the prettiest was the wife of a Southern man who made himself famous by his assaults upon slavery. She was very young and ignorant of life, but he would desert her for months, going she knew not where, to do she knew not what. He was a celebrity for a few years, but seems to have died out of public recollection.

*Page 49.*—Argruff's distinction between pride and vanity will hardly hold water, but he is not far wrong in asserting that vanity is as much a weakness of one sex as of the other.

*Page 55.*—The naval monument with the "split pitchers"—prows of ships— on its sides, has been moved, I think, to the grounds north of the Capitol.

FIFTH LETTER, *Page 59.*—"And Kanzis, Billy," It is impossible to realize at the present day the length and bitterness of the struggle over Kansas. The nominal victory achieved by the passage of the Lecompton Constitution and the English Bill was in reality a Southern defeat, presaging the disasters that were to come a few years later on the field of battle. How far away it all seems now, and what a prospect there is apparently of indefinite peace between the sections!

*Page 60.*—Mozis feels "mighty bad" about the country. He appears to have "forefelt" (is there such a word?) the inevitable struggle.

*Page 63.*—"Old Buck has tride that game." Southern men of advanced views always held that Mr. Buchanan pandered to Northern sentiment, without adequate return.

*Page 67.*—"*At presint.*" Mozis could never for a moment forget his "skeam," that was going to make him immensely rich.

*Page 68.*—"Oans' par" is alive to-day, and, far from being old, looks younger than he did twenty years ago.

SIXTH LETTER, *Page 70.*—"Cockrun's galry" was then in Mr. C.'s private residence—a mere nucleus of the present admirable gallery.

*Page 71.*—"But the Ballay," &c. Words cannot describe the effects of ballet dancing upon a young countryman who sees it for the first time. This amusement has fallen into such disrepute that it may well be believed that the American people will never again go mad as they did forty years ago over Fanny Ellsler.

*Page 75.*—"That's Dred Scot." The right of a State to reclaim a fugitive slave was tested in the United States Supreme Court in the case of Dred Scott, a famous name in consequence.

*Page 77.*—"A powful dark complected man." Prindle, or Pringle, the greatest faro-dealer of his day and generation.

SEVENTH LETTER, *Page 88.*—"Plug Uglis." So admirable is the existing police system in the United States, that one finds it hard to believe that only twenty years ago all the great cities, but especially Baltimore, and even Washington itself, the centre of government, were infested with ruffians who made night as hideous and dangerous as in London before the streets were illumined except by link-boys. The very names of these bands of outlaws, "Plug Uglies," "Blood Tubs," "Rams," &c., have lost their meaning, but they were words of terrible import to gentlefolk in Mozis's time. Most of these bands were nominally fire companies, and we owe to the steam fire engine not only exemption from conflagrations, often caused by the fire companies themselves as an excuse for rows and pillage, but a security for life and limb which could not well have been attained while these rascally organizations existed.

*Page 94.*—"Good eavnin', Miss Haryit." This letter procured for Mozis an introduction to Miss Lane and a lady friend of hers from Georgia, who was spending the winter with her at the White House. He went so far as to attend the Saturday morning receptions of Miss L., and, it is needless to say, found them exceedingly pleasant—not at all "discumboberating."

*Page 104.*—"Jawge Toun." Desperate and heart-broken over the failure of his scheme, Mozis saw Georgetown and everything else through jaundiced eyes. It is by no means the place he represents it to be.

CONCLUSION.—Half the fun as well of the writing as of the reading of "dialect" is in the bad spelling. Oftentimes the more absurd this is the better. But it mortally offends a certain class of people. When these Letters were first published, some of these people were so outraged in their delicate sensibilities that they stalked dignifiedly into print and declared that Addums was poisoning the literature of the country and depraving the public taste: as if one pitiful little bit of nonsense could emblacken the whole multitudinous sea of letters. The Rev. Mr. Hunnicutt, who was then editing a religious or perhaps a temperance paper in Fredericksburg, was so wounded that he found no relief to his aggrieved purist nature until he had bestowed upon Mozis a title more astounding even than the very worst of Mozis's misspelt words. He called him "*a mephitic jackdaw*"!